BENEVOLENT
PASSION

HEAVEN'S HEART

BENEVOLENT PASSION

BOOK TWO

AMANDA PILLAR

Published by Maatkare Books
www.amandapillar.com

Editor: Pete Kemsphall

ISBN: 978-0-6480295-7-1

Cover Design: Yocla Book Cover Designs © 2018
Internal Layout: Amanda Pillar © 2018
Editor: Pete Kempshall

First Published November 2018

To Tom—I love you.
And look what we did!

CHAPTER 1

Six Months Earlier...

Zadkiel hovered effortlessly over the Inner Sanctum, one of the most sacred areas within Heaven's Celestial City. Angels with pure white wings milled around the hall, their hair a kaleidoscope of hues, whispering amongst themselves. For many angels, this was the finale of a religious pilgrimage: the Celestial City and its mysterious artifact, Heaven's Heart, which was of such importance, it warranted twenty-four-hour protection.

He began another circuit of the hall, keeping his movements erratic and unpredictable, so if they were ever watched, no pattern would be discovered. It had been his honor to guard this immense hall and its treasure for the past two centuries, and every day he served, it reminded him of the future he had carved out for himself within his world.

Pride was meant to be a sin, but he wasn't ashamed to feel it for his achievements.

He had worked hard from the moment the threads of

silver had formed in his wings, indicating he was warrior class. He'd been younger than most when it had happened, a bare fifty years old, but he'd always known he was destined for something important, and the metallic filaments had confirmed his suspicions.

His parents had hoped he'd be a scholar or a muse, had given him a name meaning 'benevolent' in their hope that he would take after them. But God had different plans, and thankfully, they had matched Zadkiel's own. He had so desperately wanted to be a member of Heaven's army as a child, but unless your wings had silver markings, you couldn't become a warrior. And there was nothing you could do to control the presence or absence of the silver. You either were warrior class or you weren't.

Completing his final circuit, and finding nothing amiss, he swooped down to land next to Dina, the captain of their elite squadron, the Darts.

"Anything unusual?" she asked, her pale crystalline blue eyes scanning the crowd of pilgrims with fierce attention.

"No, although there appear to be fewer pilgrims today than normal."

Her wings rustled slightly as she turned, taking in the visiting angels. "Did you count how many are here?"

"Seventy-two."

"There are normally over one-hundred."

He nodded.

Her power was a steady pulse against his skin—her wings had turned almost entirely silver before he'd been born, and her golden hair was the sheen of the metal itself. There had been rumors for centuries she might ascend to archangel status one day, although she generally laughed them away whenever anyone was brave enough to repeat them to her.

But there was no denying she was commanding and beautiful, or the fact that he had once been a little bit in love with her.

Then again, Zadkiel had a feeling half the warrior class would admit to the same affliction.

"I am getting a bad feeling," Dina said, moving up next to him with an easy familiarity.

He re-examined the crowd, then walked around the squat mausoleum-like building in the middle of the hall. "I can see nothing amiss."

Dina was rubbing her chest now, a look of brutal concentration on her face. "Something is not right. I will call the others."

He stopped beside her, watching the crowd, feeling their curiosity toward the guards and their treasure, but still saw nothing wrong. However, as the youngest member of the Darts, he was nowhere near as powerful as his comrade, and he wasn't ashamed to admit it.

Dina turned cold eyes on him. "I cannot reach them."

The muscles in his jaw clenched, and he tried to send out his own telepathic query. Nothing but a gray mist met his enquiry—they had been blocked off. "How could that happen?"

"It shouldn't." Dina settled into a fighting stance, a blade of fire bursting into to life in her hand.

Zadkiel drew his own weapon, a more traditional steel-and-leather sword, not crafted by magic. It would take centuries for him to learn her skill—and even then, he may not manage to conjure a blade of fire, but rather something more pedestrian.

As long as I could summon a blade, rather than having to carry one at all times, I would be happy. Raziel could do it, as could Azrael on the odd occasion, but Seraphina and Yael, the other two members of the Darts, had yet to master the ability.

A huge booming shook the hall, causing the cloud-colored pillars to tremble and the Inner Sanctum to groan in protest. The worshippers screamed as smoke billowed into the hall, the scent of rotting flesh a pungent undertone to the burning stench.

This should not be happening.

"Could this be a test?" he asked Dina quietly.

She shook her head. "Doubtful. Even the archangels would not risk damaging Heaven's Heart for the sake of testing our defenses."

A white-winged worshipper darted close to them, his brown gaze wild with panic. "What is going on?"

Dina met his stare with a lethal one of her own. "We are under attack."

She shot into the air. "Everyone! LEAVE NOW!" Her voice echoed throughout the hall, reaching every corner.

Angels ran in all directions, some taking to the skies to avoid the crush. Zadkiel tried to ignore the panic and focused on what was creating the smoke and noise.

A second later, large powerful forms appeared in the air, their wings long and bat-like, their heads horned, and lightning billowing over their bodies.

Demons.

And not just any demons—these were Infernus, a species descended from *both* Satan and Lucifer. Horror surged through his entire body, but he didn't pause, launching into the air, and meeting one of the winged demons head on.

His sword clashed with the demon's, the blow powerful, pain wrenching through his shoulder. He ducked and dove, weaving in and out of the beast's clutches, then hacked, slicing through the tendons in his attacker's arm. Dark blood streamed from the wound, but the demon simply swapped his sword to his opposite hand, and slashed out again.

Dina's voice cut through the melee. "Watch out!"

Too late. Pain, like his skull had been split in two, ricocheted through his head and down into every limb. He spun in the air to face this new threat; another demon grinned evilly at him from a mere arm's length away.

Another blow, this from his first opponent.

Zadkiel dropped from the sky, wings barely creating enough resistance to impede his fall. He smashed into the marble floor with a brutal snapping of bones, the scent of blood and burning rising to choke him. He fought to retain his consciousness as two booted feet landed heavily next to his head.

A gravelly voice ground through his pounding head. "Nighty night, angel-boy."

Then there was nothing but darkness.

CHAPTER 2

Zadkiel was slow to come around. His head beat with a heavy rhythm, his vision was blurred, and pain echoed steadily in every inch of his body. He shut his eyes, hoping that a few more seconds of rest would improve his vision, or the agony.

It didn't.

Everything was still hazy beyond recognition, although he could make out light and dark, and that there were large shapes standing over him. Blurry, shadowy arches spread out from behind the figures' backs.

Was he surrounded by angels?

What happened? Where am I?

There was a strange antiseptic smell in the air that he associated with human medical clinics. Was he in a healer's chamber in Heaven?

Memories began to bombard him, the force of them causing his teeth to clench. There had been a problem in the hall...demons had descended on Heaven...Infernus...

Dina!

His telepathic shout hit a screen of gray mist and

vanished. One by one, he called for the other member of the Darts: Raziel, Azrael, Seraphina and Yael, but no one replied. His telepathic communication with them was still blocked.

Panic clawed at his mind; he told himself to calm down, to assess the situation. But for the first time in two centuries, he was isolated.

Truly alone.

I have to find the others. They will know what to do.

First thing, though, he needed to heal—his limbs were nothing but heavy weights, his heart laboring in his chest. Hopefully the angels surrounding him would assist him in achieving that goal in record time.

"He's awake!"

The shout made him twitch, the most movement that could be coaxed out of his slumped form.

You've been drugged. Maybe they'd had to sedate him so he could heal properly.

Or maybe your spine is broken.

He remembered pain, then falling, landing, his bones breaking with excruciating agony. He *could* have a broken spine; it would explain his slow healing. He was barely four hundred years old; still considered a baby among many of his kind. Spines—and their complicated network of nerves—took time to mend, unlike simple limb breaks.

A rough voice rumbled around the room, vaguely familiar, but not because it belonged to an angel he knew. "Give him more anesthetic."

Anesthetic?

"Boss, he's had the maximum dose."

Boss? No angel he knew was referred to as 'boss'.

"Well, he's awake and we're not done."

"He's paralyzed still."

A pause. Then that deep voice again. "Fine. But be quick."

Footsteps echoed as one of the shadows walked away. Then the Boss spoke, but his voice was quieter. "I have to go meet the others. Finish the job."

Tiny aching bursts spread from Zadkiel's wings, the discomfort sizzling along nerves that were fighting back to life.

The realization was swift and brutal. *They're plucking my wings.*

Despair settled heavy on his body. He was not being tended to by angels.

It's the Infernus.

They must have taken him.

But what had happened to Dina? To the other Darts? Why weren't they answering him?

More starbursts of pain. Angel feathers sold for a small fortune on the black-market, as they were almost impossible to come by. It wasn't like angels gave them up freely. Worse, demons especially loved them, because they could be used for forbidden spells.

This isn't happening.

But it was.

He'd been warned about torture—had trained for it—but he'd never imagined being paralyzed from the neck down yet still able to *feel*, to know he was being treated as nothing more than a deceased bird being readied for the roasting pan.

A sharp slice of pain down his abdomen made him open his eyes, but he could still see nothing except blurred images. Blood drenched the air with the scent of iron.

"What are you doing?" someone asked.

"I've heard angel organs sell for a bomb."

"We're just meant to be taking the feathers." Sharp pricks of pain accompanied the words as yet more feathers were stolen. A shadowy limb held something out in front of them. "These are pretty."

"*Pretty*?"

"What?" The question was defensive. "They have silver through them. My cub would love them."

"Ever since you spawned you haven't been the same."

"Says a cub-less male."

"I have the right priorities."

"Like pissing off the boss?"

"He won't know."

"You've just sliced the damned angel from navel to sternum. You think he won't notice that?"

"It will heal."

"Since none of the feathers have grown back, I'm not sure about that."

His feathers weren't growing back?

Then a new, deeper pain erupted through his body, and he passed out with a groan.

"What in Satan's holy balls did you do to the angel?" The deep-voiced shout snapped Zadkiel awake. His wings burned, and his abdomen felt like someone had rifled through his organs. The scent of blood was rich and pervasive.

"Just took a bit of his liver."

"It looks like it's dying."

"Maybe their wings have magic and we took too many feathers—"

"*Of course* their wings have magic. That's why you were harvesting them, you fucking idiot. A dead angel is no good to me."

"The liver will grow back. Does for demons all the time. I think it even does in humans."

There was the sound of flesh hitting flesh, and bone snapping. "I don't pay you to fucking think. I give you a task, and you stick to it."

"Yes, Boss." The words were mumbled, as if through a bruised mouth.

Something touched his wings then. A scream built in his throat, but he locked his jaw; he would not let them know of his pain.

"The feathers aren't regenerating."

"The angel is weak. He might have suffered an injury when you captured him. It seems to be hindering his healing abilities."

"Hmm."

Shouts sounded somewhere distant.

"Motherfucker. I had better go see what the fuss is about."

Another tug on his wing, this one forcing out the scream he'd kept bottled.

"Keep the angel alive."

Zadkiel woke with a start, his entire body throbbing in time to the blood pounding through his skull. No change in his condition, at least, none that he could detect. His limbs were still frozen and his wings felt raw. And he still couldn't see.

The others will come for me. They will.

All he had to do was stay alive.

"Those fucking assholes think they can play me?!"

Re-opening his eyes, he tried to focus on something, *anything*, but it was just darkness and light.

I think I have a brain injury. It would explain the loss of vision, and why his body wasn't healing his wings or half-destroyed liver—it was prioritizing the head injury.

"Boss?"

"I will not be played."

"No, Boss."

"Those fuckers are going to pay for trying to screw me over."

"Yes, Boss."

Something bumped against Zadkiel's side, and a finger ran down his stomach, over his stitched wound. "Angel-boy, your life has just become very important to me."

He tried to focus on the speaker, but all he could make out was a dark blob with large protuberances on his head.

That was when the pain really began.

CHAPTER 3

Five months later...

Peony Marshall sat in front of her computer with a sigh, her bones aching and her body sore. She'd been on her feet for the past twelve hours, trying to save the life of a gray-skinned Brevine demon that had been clawed up while trying to steal from a fellow assassin.

Most members of the Halcyon Guild did not take kindly to theft from their comrades. Theft from their enemies? Well, the more brazen you were, the more kudos to you.

Their boss—or slave master, depending on how you wanted to see it—had been furious. Trick had ordered Peony's treatment to be more painful than necessary, a demand she had promptly ignored. She worked her slave-debt off by saving lives, not by making people hurt. That was her identical twin's job.

The Skype ringtone sounded from her computer, and she answered with a weary sigh. "Hi, Mom."

The video kicked in, and Peony stared at the face of

her adopted mother, Selene. As ever, a mix of happiness-pain burned in her chest. She'd always known she was adopted—the fact that her mother was green-eyed and dark-haired in comparison to Peony's white hair and golden skin was a bit of a giveaway. Oh, and they were totally different species.

But Peony had been born free, whereas her sister had been sold into slavery as a newborn. That meant Peony's reaction to her mother varied: gratitude that she'd had the life she had, sadness that her mother hadn't stepped in to save Dru as well; remorse for the pain that Dru had brought into their lives, and guilt for having chosen to leave her mom to pick up the pieces on her own.

"Sweetheart, you look tired." Her mother's voice was light and comforting, a delicate frown on her face. She looked more like Peony's sister, rather than mother.

"Long night with a foolish demon," Peony replied.

"What happened?"

"You know I can't really talk about guild business." Fact was, Peony probably *could* talk about it, but she didn't want her mother to know much about her new life. Some things were better left unsaid.

And it was always better to keep her mother happy.

Selene tsked. "Demons are always so violent."

"*Mom*."

She flicked a mass of raven-dark hair over her shoulder. "What? They are."

"*You're* part demon."

And Peony was half-demon, half-human. A cambion. It was too bad for her that her demon genes were stronger than her human ones.

Selene smiled and held up her forefinger and thumb

about an inch apart. "Only a little bit."

Peony didn't really want to have a debate about their respective genealogies. Her mother wasn't a cambion, though. You had to be half-human to earn that hated title.

"How's work?" Peony asked, changing the topic to something Selene was always happy to discuss.

"Busy as always." Her mother was a nurse, and she was employed at a thriving human hospital. She did a lot of ER work nowadays, to try to filter out the demons that were accidentally sent to human institutions; sort of an advanced-guard for the supernatural. It helped avoid the discovery of 'medical miracles' and rare deformities.

It was her mother who'd inspired her to get into medicine. Because even though Selene worked as nurse, she was qualified in almost every medical field you could imagine. That's what happened when you were immortal and could afford to start a new life every two decades or so. Peony had loved that her mother was so smart, and that she'd dedicated her numerous lifetimes to saving other people. Peony had thought that she could do the same thing, but she had a few fundamental differences that made her goals impossible.

I was an idiot.

Her mother's voice cut through her musing. "Did you get my care package?"

"Yes, thanks. I ate it already." Peony had a sweet tooth that would put most people to shame—and Selene indulged it brazenly. "I really liked the donuts," she added.

"I bought them from this charming little—"

A knock on the door made Peony turn in her chair.

"You get that," Selene said. "We can talk again later."

"Okay."

"Say hi to your sister for me."

"Will do," she lied.

"Love you."

"You, too."

She disconnected the call. Standing, she made sure her gloves were pulled up, and that her sleeves and trousers covered any bare skin. There was no way she was going to pass on her mother's regards to her sister. Dru could barely tolerate the Christmas cards that Selene sent her, although Peony wasn't entirely sure why her sister found the little pieces of paper so offensive. Dru had been stolen from the hospital before Peony's adopted mom could have saved her, but maybe her sister hated Selene nonetheless.

Opening the door, Peony's spine locked at the sight of her boss on the other side. Trick gave her a once-over, his brown gaze condescending. He didn't really like her, but that was fine, because the feeling was mutual.

Peony had trained to be a healer, and this man profited from death.

He finished his visual assessment. "You look like shit."

"Thanks." She resisted the urge to poke out her tongue.

"I need you."

"Sorry, I don't do that kind of house-call." She needed to watch herself, to not annoy him too much. Trick was *powerful* and he wasn't known for being a relaxed slave master. You couldn't be, not when you controlled a den of assassins who could as easily cut your throat as take your orders. But it was a well-known fact in the guild that

Trick was keen to try his luck with Dru, and since she and Peony looked identical...

"You wish," he snorted, then spun on his heel and walked back down the corridor.

She shut the door and followed him. "No, not really."

Sure, Trick was a handsome bastard—all golden hair, dreamy brown eyes, and a body that most women wanted to climb—but he wasn't her type. *Demons* weren't her type. Neither were humans or anyone else. But that was another story.

Trick led the way through the maze of halls and corridors that made up the guild's main headquarters, toward an office he barely used. He paused outside the door. "If you ever tell anyone about what you see or hear in this meeting, your life is forfeit. Understand?"

She came to full awareness, as if she'd been doused with a bucket of cold water. "Yes. But my contract—"

"Your life is owed to me. You can buy it back, or you can forfeit it. That's how the system works. Don't tattle on what you hear today, and you won't die. Simple."

She swallowed. She'd always kind of thought of the blood-contract as a loan—she loaned her life to Trick until she paid off her debt, then she got her soul back and everything was done and dusted.

I probably should have read the fine print more closely.

And normally, she would have done. Her mother had always taught her to pay attention to the small details, because it was often these that gave clues about what was wrong with an individual. But the day she'd agreed to hand her soul over to Trick had been one of the worst in her life, and she hadn't really been all that aware...

"You going to come in or just stand there?" Trick's

voice snapped her back to the present.

I must be more tired than I thought. She didn't normally stand daydreaming in hallways.

In fact, she'd stopped daydreaming a long time ago.

Following him inside, he waved her to a dim corner, where she took up position against a wall. His face was set hard as stone as he scanned the room, then nodded to himself. He strode behind his desk—one of the two pieces of furniture—and clicked his fingers.

The sizzle of electricity filled the space, and then it burst with a pop, leaving the skin on her face—the only exposed part of her—feeling raw. Two huge demons now occupied the room, holding up an unconscious man with tattered, bony wings, a hand under each of his armpits. Electricity crackled over their skin, and they shook themselves, bat-like wings rustling.

Infernus.

She hadn't ever seen these horned creatures before in real life—Hell, her knowledge about most demon species was pretty sketchy—but she'd heard about them. Children of both Lucifer and Satan, they were evil to the bone. And proud of it.

Her fingers itched to help the slumped man, but she kept her position against the wall. If she disobeyed Trick now, things wouldn't end well for her. She didn't need a warning from him to say as much.

"What have you brought me, Kerrington?" Trick's voice was full of ennui.

The taller of the two Infernus stepped forward, letting go of his hold on the man, who drooped heavily. A dark voice filled the room. "An angel."

Did he just say...?

Trick raised a golden eyebrow. "Really? It looks like you've flayed the skin off a human and then stuck some bones on its back."

"I promise you, it's an angel."

Trick tilted his head to one side, skepticism lining his features. "It doesn't look...well."

"There was a bit of a problem," Kerrington agreed, as if the man had just encountered some bad traffic and not been tortured.

"You plucked it."

"Its feathers are worth money."

"They haven't grown back."

"It's young. They will."

"This significantly decreases its value."

Kerrington spluttered. "When it heals—"

"Of which there is no guarantee." Trick walked around his desk and squatted next to the angel, poking it every now and then with his index finger.

An angel. Wow.

Peony may not like Trick, but she respected his knowledge; the guild leader had been doing his job a *lot* longer than she had been alive. If he believed the man was an angel, then he must be.

A shrug from the huge demon. "It's an angel, they heal."

"Peony!"

She jerked a little at her name, but stood straight and nodded at Trick. He gestured for her to come closer.

"Inspect this."

This. Not him. *Way to dehumanize someone.*

Oh wait, demons weren't human, and neither were angels.

She tried to ignore the two hulking figures that loomed on either side of her as her gloved fingers carefully worked over the parts of the angel she could reach.

"What is the woman doing?"

"The woman is my medical professional."

That was probably the kindest thing Trick had ever said about her.

"Can you please place him on the floor?"

The Infernus simply let go of the man, and she lurched forward to catch him before he slammed face-first onto the carpet. She glared at the demon. "Carefully next time."

A mucusy snort was her only reply.

"You have women doing medical work for you?" Incredulity laced Kerrington's voice.

The man smelled strongly of antiseptic and blood. *Cranium feels spongy—probably a depressed fracture on the parietal bone.*

"I have women do all kinds of things for me," Trick murmured.

Eww.

At least she knew that Dru only murdered for him.

Wings are almost destroyed. All feathers have been removed. Tendons and sinews exposed, bone exposed, not broken. She didn't know the medical terms for angel-wing bones. Birds had radii and ulnas—but they didn't have arms.

The demon shook his head. "Women don't do the dirty work. That's men's business."

Spine may have been damaged, too difficult to tell without an X-ray. She moved on to his arms and legs. *Superior and inferior extremities intact.*

"I am not from your archaic background. So deal." Trick shrugged.

"I need to roll him on his side, so I can check his anterior," Peony interrupted. Blank stares met her request. "I need to check his front," she clarified, her voice firm and strong. Confident. It was the kind of tone she used to use when working in the hospital; people would react to her authority without even realizing it.

The second demon squatted next to her, the faint scent of roses reaching her.

How strange.

"We need to do this gently," she warned him. "I don't want to damage his wings more than they are already."

A nod. "Okay."

Together they rolled him into something resembling the recovery position, and she began checking his vitals without any of her equipment. *Would have been nice if he'd told me I was going to be doing this.* She could have at least brought her blood pressure cuff and stethoscope.

From what she could determine, his pulse was erratic; he'd had someone cut into his stomach, and his head had been shaved roughly, leaving smears of blood over his fractured skull. She stood.

"I don't know much about angelic recuperative powers, but if he was a human, he'd be dead," Peony said.

"What did you find?" Trick asked.

Remember to use plain English, she told herself. Trick got impatient with 'medical jargon'. "Broken skull, possible broken spine, wings are destroyed, someone's cut him open—did you take any organs?" She directed the last at the gravel-voiced Infernus.

"No comment."

She focused on Trick. "Organs have been harvested. It's lucky he's still breathing."

"So, you want me to buy a half-dead angel with limited hope of recovery?" Trick asked the demons.

"She didn't say that it wouldn't recover."

"I give about a ten percent chance," Peony said. "Since he hasn't started regenerating on his own, he will need all the help he can get."

And she hoped she was the one to give it.

CHAPTER 4

If Trick doesn't buy this guy, he's doomed.

She'd learned that there weren't too many demon-healers out there—most demons preferred to kill—and while the man's angel-buddies could probably help him, she seriously doubted that the Infernus would be willing to sell him back to Heaven. They'd be signing their own death warrants; the angels would slaughter whoever approached them, then take their buddy back, anyway.

"Ten percent chance of survival?" Trick tsked as he stared down his nose at the broken angel. "That also dramatically lowers the price."

Kerrington spluttered. "It's an *angel*. It will live. And they're *rare*."

"So, you didn't pluck every feather from his body? And you *didn't* harvest any organs?" Or beat him to within an inch of his life?" Peony's voice was surprisingly calm, despite the churning in her gut.

She'd been living with demons for a decade now, and she still didn't understand the random viciousness or the brutality of their world. Sure, she'd grown up in the

Human Realm and had trained as a doctor; she'd seen violence, but the nature of it was different in Hell. And she'd only been to Tartarus—she could only imagine what it was like in the realms ruled by Satan and Lucifer.

The huge demon stared at her. "Angels regenerate. It's a fact. This," he waved a hand at the prone male, "is nothing."

"Then why hasn't he started to heal yet, if they regenerate so well?"

The demon's black eyes narrowed. "I don't know."

"Then you don't know for sure that he *will* heal on his own, without medical intervention?"

Kerrington gritted his teeth. "No."

Then without her help—or that of another medical professional—the angel was a dead man. And she didn't want to see him die: she hated losing any of her patients, despite the fact that the majority of them were hired killers.

Do no harm.

Funny, how the Hippocratic Oath nor Lasagna's Oath—the new, updated version—didn't mention that line at all, but it had formed part of her training for as long as she could remember. Her mother had been especially strict on the concept.

"This is going to seriously affect your asking price," Trick said.

Peony hadn't pointed out the medical facts just so that he could buy the angel more cheaply, but Trick was a business man, and to him, this angel's life was nothing more than a business transaction.

We're all chess pieces to him.

Hell, he'd probably value a nice chess set *more*.

It didn't matter. What mattered was that he bought the angel so she could save him.

"When its wings grow back, you will have all the feathers you want." Kerrington's black eyes glinted.

Trick crossed his arms over his chest. "Angel wings lose their potency in Hell. The longer an angel is in Hell, the less value its feathers hold. Everyone knows that."

Peony hadn't known that.

Kerrington's jaw clenched. "They are still angel feathers."

"Worth far less than what you just harvested."

Peony fought to keep her face expressionless as her slave-master and the Infernus demon haggled. This was a man's *life* they were talking about—and it meant less than nothing to either of them, except in commercial value.

The angel groaned. Was he waking?

Before Peony could move, the fallen man shot an arm out, gripping the second Infernus demon's leg. Kerrington scowled, then kicked out.

No.

Without thinking, Peony jumped in the way of the blow, letting out an *oomph* when the huge booted foot contacted her shin, hard. Pain radiated up her leg, and she bit the inside of her cheek to keep from moaning. She shifted her weight to her right foot, easing some of the pressure off her injured limb.

I'm going to struggle to walk after this.

Sure, she healed fast, but she could already feel the lump forming on her shin.

Imagine if that blow had landed on the angel...

"What the Hell do you think you're doing?" Trick's

voice sliced through the room.

He closed on Kerrington, stopping barely a foot from the huge demon and facing off against him. For a split second, she worried about what would happen, then realized that Trick and the demon were evenly matched, physically anyway. She'd always thought of her boss as elegant and lithe, but in reality, he was as tall as the Infernus—minus the horns—and just as muscular under his suit.

"The angel was waking up—"

"You just touched *my property*." Trick's brown eyes burned.

Oh. He's talking about me.

"She stepped in the way—"

"You did not have permission to use force against one of my slaves. And you almost damaged my potential property, hindering its healing progress even more. I could cut your throat for the first offence alone."

Power built in the room, the magic a steady pulse against her skin.

And it was coming from Trick.

She hadn't realized he was *that* powerful. *I don't even know what kind of demon he* is. In fact, none of the Halcyon Guild knew what their master was. She figured the secret was a ploy on her boss' part to keep people on their toes.

For the first time, Kerrington's meanness abated, and something like fear crept into his gaze.

The second Infernus kicked the angel's hand away and stepped back, distancing himself from both the angel and Peony.

"If she hadn't stepped in the way..."

"Don't blame my slave for your actions."

"But—"

"You either sell me the angel now, or leave. It's up to you."

"I can sell the angel elsewhere..."

Trick leaned his hip against the desk. "Then do it."

Tense silence filled the room.

Kerrington cursed. "I need the option of buying the angel back."

Trick's dark-blond eyebrows rose. "You want me to buy a slave and then sell it back to you? Like I run a fucking a pawn shop?"

A deep sigh. "It needs medical help and we hear you are equipped to deal with it."

"I won't sell it back to you for what I pay you today. If it heals, there'll be a lot of work that went into it, and medical assistance isn't cheap. And who knows? I may want to keep it afterwards. Haven't had an angel blood slave before."

"Fine, as long as the option is there."

"Ten million dollars," Trick said.

Kerrington stepped back and thrust his chin up, indicating his compatriot to follow suit. They spoke in low tones for a few minutes.

Peony couldn't believe it. If ten million dollars was *cheap*, what on earth were angels worth in perfect health, with all their feathers?

I wasn't worth that much.

No, but then, no one was sure how long she'd live, so they'd agreed on a price she could work off in a lifetime.

"I agree to the terms," the demon said.

Trick clapped his hands together. "Let's get the paperwork signed." He shot Peony a look, which she interpreted to mean 'go back to your corner'.

She concentrated on not limping, wincing as she headed back to the wall. Then she slowly turned on her good leg and watched as knives were drawn, bank account details given, and paperwork signed in blood. Kerrington roughly grabbed the angel's thumb, nicked it, then used the blood to place a fingerprint on the contract.

Did it count as a real contract if the signatory was unconscious?

She was desperate to help the angel, but she stayed where she was; considering he hadn't died from his injuries yet, she figured a few more minutes might not hurt. If this had been a hospital, though, she'd have been working on him the instant he came into view.

"It is done." Trick tapped the signed papers against his desk, then he looked over at the two Infernus. "If I see either you of you in the next year, though, you're dead."

Kerrington spluttered. "We have first right to buy—"

"Yes, but I won't be selling this angel to *anyone* until it's healed. And considering you touched my property without permission, you're lucky I agreed to this deal. So get out, and stay away from me. Or—" Power sizzled through the room again.

"Or what?"

Trick nodded at Kerrington's companion, who screamed, a horrible high-pitched sound. His muscles bunched, and his head thrashed from side to side, before the sound cut off suddenly. The scent of singed roses filled the room, making her want to gag. A second later, the demon went limp, the electrical pulses that had flickered on his skin from the moment he entered, gone.

"That is just a taste of what I can do. Don't piss me off,

and you don't need to know what I do to those who really annoy me."

Kerrington's mouth pressed into a thin line. "Point taken."

Somehow, she doubted it was. Resolve was etched into every line of the demon's body.

"Let's go."

With a crackle of magic, the two demons teleported away.

Trick bent down and examined the angel's torso, before pressing his open hand on the bare skin. A low moan filled the room, like the angel was in pain.

"What did you do?" Peony demanded angrily, ready to dive between Trick and her new patient.

"I've branded him—it's what happens when someone becomes a blood slave."

She'd never heard of that before. "I don't have one."

"No. But then, touching him won't kill me." He sighed. "Wait here."

Like she was going to leave the angel, but she kept her mouth shut.

Trick walked to the opposite wall, then tapped a random series of stone bricks. A doorway opened before him, the dark interior swallowing his frame as he disappeared.

Hidden tunnels, why am I not surprised?

He was probably spying on everything.

There's no probably about it.

Funny how her inner voice suddenly sounded like Dru. Her sister was convinced Trick tracked their movements, to the point that she had paid a small fortune to lay spells in her room to counter just such prying.

Guessing Trick would be back when he felt like it, Peony limped over to the angel, then kneeled on the ground, hissing as the egg on her shin made contact with the floor. She redid her preliminary exam, coming to the same conclusions as before.

He'd really benefit from some rehydration, antibiotics, and pain relief. That said, she wasn't sure that antibiotics would work on an angel. She had a rather poor track record with her patients reacting to the medication—anaphylaxis had been the least of her problems.

Trick's voice came from over her shoulder. "Any improvement?"

She jumped, and hissed as her shin jerked against the ground. "No."

The golden-haired demon had wheeled in a gurney. *Did he just raid my clinic?* Although, 'clinic' was really a euphemism for the box of a room and minimal supplies she'd been given.

"Let's move him out of my office."

Peony stood. "To the clinic?"

"No. I don't want anyone knowing we have an angel here."

She frowned. "Why?"

His expression closed. "Because while the assassins here are largely slaves, they still have free will. And many of them have grudges against angels. Until I'm ready for this to become public knowledge, it stays a secret. Got it?"

Peony nodded. She was entirely sure she bought his story, but angels and demons weren't exactly friends, so the rivalry was clear.

"Now, let's get him sorted."

As she turned back to the angel, her body stiffened. He

was looking right at her, with eyes of the purest green she'd ever seen. It was like he could see straight into her soul.

And what he saw there concerned him.

CHAPTER 5

Pain.

Zadkiel's whole body screamed with it. His head and wings hurt the most, the sensation akin to razor blades slicing along his flesh. But at least he could no longer smell that strange combination of antiseptic and blood.

"Careful!"

He didn't recognize the voice.

Opening his eyes, the first thing he noticed was that he could see properly again. Earlier, harsh shadows had clouded his sight. Now, his gaze traced over a shock of white hair that contrasted sharply with golden-hued skin. The scent of sugar reached him.

It was a woman.

No.

As his other senses kicked in, he realized that the stranger was a *demon*. Not a woman, not a *person*.

Another Hell-spawn.

Although, while he had no idea what kind of demon she was, she certainly *wasn't* Infernus.

"Damnit, Trick! I said be careful!" Her gray eyes

blazed at something behind him, and he realized he was being lifted off a bed by someone he couldn't see. His nerves fired at being moved, the agony spearing through him, but he stayed conscious, miracle of miracles.

He was placed rather unceremoniously on a hard bench, face down. His cheek pressed roughly against what might be a towel, the faint smell of flowers drifting from the fabric.

Then someone was touching his wings. He wanted to fight the hands, to shove them away, but his limbs would not respond. *Paralyzed again.* But this felt different to last time, like a wound that hadn't healed, rather than a drug forced on him.

Why can I feel my limbs, but not move them?

The hands that explored his withered wings were gentle, professional almost, in their movements. While the demon female worked, he wondered if he should risk calling mentally for the other Darts. Would the telepathy be tracked? *You don't know until you try.* He blocked out the feel of hands moving over him, and concentrated on Dina, then the others. Nothing. Just the gray mist.

Maybe the wounds to my head have impacted on my ability. Or he was just too far away. That thought brought him little comfort.

"How bad is it?" The voice was male, not one he recognized.

"His wings are in pretty bad shape. It looks like the sores are infected, and the wounds just aren't healing. I don't think this was done recently." The demon woman moved into his line of sight as she investigated the arches of his wings. She was covered from neck to toe in blue clothing, like something he might see in a human hospital.

Where am I?

He could only hear and smell the two people already in the room. There was no sign of the Infernus.

"How long do you think he's been like this?" the unseen male asked.

'He' *is awake.*

But did he really want to interact with these demons? They could be worse than the Infernus, lulling him into a false sense of security. Skies, they could just be the Infernus' lackeys, and he would be in for more pain as soon as they were done investigating his wounds.

"If this was a human, I'd say a week or two. But the time it would take for disease like this to infect a demon? It could have been months. I have no idea for angels. However, his immune system does appear to have been compromised. So that might account for the state of his health. Could the removal of his feathers have done it?"

He wanted to snort at her ignorance. Angel feathers weren't magical, at least, not like that. They were like a bird's—good for flying.

"Doubtful," the male replied. "The value of angel feathers isn't tied to their healing properties—it's associated with the fact that angelic energy can fuel demonic spells."

How did he know that?

But he answered his own question: *He's a demon. And angel feathers have been hunted for a long time. Don't be stupid.*

His head wound must be affecting him more than he realized.

"I see." Her reply was cool and slightly disapproving.

Of which part? he wondered.

Her hands shifted from their investigation of his wings, to his head, back and legs. "I can't diagnose him properly without an X-ray machine, but I think he has a fractured skull and spine."

That would explain why he had lost control of his limbs. Although, why he wasn't totally numb was odd. Considering the torture, his body was probably in overload.

Maybe you are *healing, just very slowly.*

"What if we ask Opal to have a look?" the female suggested.

"No one can know about him. And you know Opal, she'll take one look at his emaciated frame and fall in love."

The hands paused in their perusal. "Her relationship record isn't very good, that's true."

What kind of a demon was Opal that she be able to diagnose what plagued him? He assumed she was a demon, and not a human or angel.

No angel would work with a group of demons.

Not even if it was in their best interests.

A starburst of pain shot through his skull as the woman's fingers carefully assessed his wound again. "I think this has partially healed since it was first inflicted."

"So, he *is* healing?"

"I think so. But he looks like he's been poisoned. Everywhere I've touched has bruised. I could really do with taking some bloods and—"

"We've been over this. I can't afford to buy you everything you 'need'."

"You paid ten million dollars for *him*. Some of this

equipment—"

"Is a complete waste of money. Work with what you have. Get some spells or other demons to help fill in the blanks. Although, run any request for demonic assistance by me first. I will approve access. I am running an assassination guild here, not a fucking hospital."

Zadkiel was at a guild?

He'd heard of them, of course. They were considered by angelkind to be some of the worst hotbeds of demonic rage and trouble: a demon could get anything they wanted from these dens of iniquity, for a price. And now he was in one? Or near one of the masters?

This really wasn't good.

Is it worse than the Infernus?

That he wasn't sure about.

And if he was here, where was Dina? Had she been brought here, too? He wanted to ask the question, but when he opened his mouth, nothing but a croak emerged.

"You're awake!" The startled comment had him raising his chin, meeting the stare of the female demon. She seemed taken aback for a moment, before turning away from him, like his gaze had burned her. "He needs water, and I think I should cannulate him..."

"Fine. Get your supplies."

She hurried out of sight, a door closing.

His stomach clenched, but no new pain arrived after her departure.

So, she wasn't the only thing stopping this male from hurting me.

A few seconds later, a demon strode into view, before dropping to a squat, so they were at eye-level. He was wearing a suit and had shiny blond hair and dark-brown eyes. He was classically handsome, with no outward signs of his demonic ancestry. He could pass for a human, or a wingless angel, for that matter.

This must be the guild master.

Funny, he didn't look like a killer. But then, looks were often deceiving.

"What's your name?" the stranger asked.

He didn't reply.

Part of him wondered if he was even entitled to his name anymore. He'd been gone from Heaven, taken, and surely that meant he was no longer able to serve, even if he were to gain his freedom. Who would want an angel with his track record on their team?

No one he knew.

After all, his commission on the Darts had been something special. Sure, some said the team's role was largely ceremonial, but Dina was a powerhouse, and she'd been running the Darts for centuries. No one doubted her skill or achievements. And it had made sense for the best of the best to guard one of Heaven's most treasured artifacts.

Did they take it? he wondered. Or had the others arrived to prevent the theft? He hoped Dina and the rest of the Darts were out searching for him, that the Heart had been kept safe.

"Hello?" The man clicked his fingers in front of Zadkiel's face. "Are you listening?"

He managed a raspy, "Yes." He had the feeling that if he ignored this guild master, things wouldn't go well for him.

"What's your name?"

He didn't want to give this demon his real name—and

he wasn't even sure if he was a true angel anymore. It wasn't like he had the wings to prove it.

"Z."

The male's face looked skeptical, but then he shrugged. "Fine. Z, my name is Trick. I am your master."

The demon spoke the truth, but how could that be? Had his ability to sense lies been damaged?

"M-m-master?" He launched into a coughing fit, agony shooting through his body at the convulsions.

The demon waited patiently for his coughing to subside. "You were sold to me today, by a group of Infernus. Ring any bells?"

The sale? No. But the Infernus...

"Where...am...I?"

"Tartarus. In the Halcyon Guild." A cold, hard smile bloomed on Trick's face. The expression was anything but happy. "It's your new home."

He was in *Hell?*

But it made sense. Where else would you hide an angel? The Human Realm would be too risky.

"What...?" His throat was too dry to finish the question.

"This is an assassination guild, but we offer a range of services to our clients. I've not had an angel blood slave before, so I'd try and heal quickly if I were you, before my patience runs out."

Blood slave...

"My wings—"

Trick clucked. "Are in very poor shape. If they don't heal, I'll remove them."

No!

The demon must have seen the horror on his face, and

gave Z's cheek a light, condescending pat. "No wings are better than half-rotten bits of bone that will kill you from infection."

The rationale almost sounded...legitimate.

But I can't lose them.

He was so young, if this demon took his wings, they might never grow back. The older and more powerful the angel, the harder the removal was. Some were said to be so powerful, only an archangel's sword could do the deed.

But he wasn't in that category.

And now he was in Hell. Both literally and figuratively.

If he didn't heal—

"I'm back!" The demon woman sounded breathless. She hurried over, brushing past Trick and hauling a cart after her. She grabbed a plastic cup of water and a straw in one hand, and then glared at the blond demon until he moved out of the way.

"Here." She bent down and held the cup in front of Zadkiel—no, Z. "Have a drink. But slowly, you don't want to choke."

He met her gray gaze and froze. There was kindness there. Real kindness. In his surprise he obeyed, the water a cool blessing as it slid down his parched throat.

"Good." She waited until he finished, then went back to the cart.

"I'm going to head back to the hall. Do what you can." Trick then turned his attention to Z. "Do what she says, and heal as quickly as possible. Otherwise, remember what I said."

Then he was gone.

"Don't mind him," the woman said. "He likes to be dramatic. Now, let's get some antiseptic on those wings."

Then a whole new kind of torture began.

CHAPTER 6

She dreamed of emerald green, the color so pure she'd never seen its like before. Wonder, excitement and—strangely—attraction pulsed through her as she took in the particular shade.

When she woke, she stared at the black ceiling for a solid ten minutes, berating herself. She *had* seen that color green before: in the angel's eyes.

That was not good.

He was just a patient.

That was it.

Sure, keep telling yourself that.

But she'd always been fascinated with things that were meant to be 'good'. And meeting an angel in real life? Well, you couldn't get much closer to 'good' than that.

Mom will be annoyed.

That was true. Her mother didn't trust angels, didn't trust anyone, really. Selene used her medical abilities to weed out the demons from her ER and prevent humans from learning the truth about them. She didn't enjoy healing her demonic brethren, just did it so they wouldn't have an excuse to hang around the hospital. And she'd always been dismissive of angels.

But that is because Mom has some...hang-ups.

Oh, Selene had endless patience for humans, which Peony found a little strange, considering all the damage they'd caused their world. But that was another issue. When it came to demons and angels, though? Selene couldn't get away quick enough.

She shouldn't think about her mother. It just made the homesick ache in her chest worse.

She didn't regret her decision to sign on to the Halcyon Guild, wouldn't ever, but she hadn't wanted to leave home and everything she'd built there. Plus, her mom had been her best friend. Sure, there was her sister—and they had each other now—but Dru wasn't BFF material.

Time to get up.

She didn't want to, though. That was unusual. Even after she'd signed her soul over to Trick, she'd been proactive about joining in life here at the guild. She'd made her bed, and she'd lie in it. Except now, she didn't really want to leave it.

With a sigh, she dragged the sheets away, and swung her legs over the edge of the mattress. The cold floor made her exhale sharply.

I should start wearing socks to bed.

She knew she wouldn't. Her room, with the door locked, was the only place in her life where she didn't have to cover herself in clothing from neck to toe. The only time she didn't have to worry about hurting someone accidentally.

Peony ducked into her small ensuite—apparently she was 'lucky' she didn't have to use a communal bathroom—and quickly washed. Then she dressed, braided her white hair and stared at her bare hands for a few seconds, a feeling of resentment welling deep within her, before going to choose a pair of gloves.

If gloves were shoes, most women would envy her collection. Peony hated wearing them, though. She did it because she wasn't a murderer by nature and she'd promised herself that she'd never, ever, kill someone.

Peony might have toxic skin, but she wasn't going to be defined by it.

After picking out a red leather pair of gloves, she left her room and locked the door. She couldn't be too careful, especially since the other guild members had taken to stealing from each other. Not that she *had* anything worth taking, other than her computer, but demons were weird. She might find her entire glove collection gone.

Her stomach rumbled ominously as she turned down the hallway. Glancing at her watch, she decided that she would check on her secret patient later. Trick had been on night duty, and since he hadn't texted her with an emergency, she assumed everything was okay.

You know he'd lie straight to your face.

Not about a ten million-dollar asset, though.

That thought, she could trust. If there was one thing in this world that Trick loved, it was money. And he hated losing it.

Therefore, it was breakfast time.

Heading to the mess, she found the corridors largely empty. That wasn't strange in itself; the guild's members tended to work odd hours. Apparently, there was a lot of delicate timing involved with thieving, spying and killing.

All Peony knew was that being a doctor had meant working twenty-four-seven. No delicate timing there—it was all hands on deck, all the time. Some days, she really missed it. Other days, well, she liked the challenge of her new job, not that she admitted that to her mother. Patching up demons—assassins, too—wouldn't be high on her parent's triage list.

The mess was largely empty when she arrived, which suited her. She could eat quickly, without having one of her co-workers corner her to look at their strange rashes or the boils on their backs or, worse, ask "Are my genitalia normal?". She never wanted to see Errant's penis again. Sure, he was an excellent administrator and bookkeeper, but he had trouble keeping his dick out of infected demon prostitutes.

It had been gross.

She made herself think of kittens and puppies, otherwise she wouldn't be able to stomach any food. Looking at the metal-and-glass food-warmer, however, she saw just a range of meat products without even any scrambled eggs or hash browns to serve as side dishes.

Billy must be on duty. The Ulnak demon was a carnivore and had little patience for anything that couldn't be sliced off a bone.

Turning away, she spotted some yogurt, cereal and fruit that had been shoved in the corner on a small side table, like an afterthought. She made herself a bowl of yogurt and peaches, and then stared at the cereal boxes. Cheerios, granola, and Fruit Loops. The logical choice would be granola, since she could just add it to her bowl, but...

She was eating her first mouthful of Fruit Loops when Sylvester and Metcalf plonked down in front of her. The two men had plates full of meat, with Sylvester having added a single grape to his meal. There wasn't a carbohydrate in sight in Metcalf's breakfast, but then he was a Reynard's Imp, and they were carnivores through and through.

Metcalf gave her a toothy smile and clicked one of his claws against the scarred tabletop. His nose had been broken—badly—and it was something they'd bonded over. "Fruit Loops, Doc? Really?"

Peony sighed. She should have known someone would catch her. But she loved sugar, and she'd already eaten all the yummy things from her mom's care package. "Glucose is good for energy."

"But not for the waistline!" Opal waved as she passed, carrying a leg of lamb all to herself. She was tall, painfully thin, and was wearing a jacket that looked like it was probably lead-lined. "Hey, Doc!"

Sylvester rolled his eyes. "Don't worry about Opal. You know Radiato demons. They think anything more than skin and bone is unattractive."

"Thanks. But I wasn't particularly worried." Being a cambion meant that she had a high-speed metabolism. She could, and did, eat pretty much anything she wanted. Too bad for her most of it involved desserts, which weren't so easy to come by in Tartarus.

Man, I would love a Snickers bar right now.

"Good, because you don't need to worry." Sylvester gave her a boyish grin that belied the fact he was one of the best thieves in the guild.

He was also so pretty it was almost shocking, with his baby blue eyes, chestnut hair and killer body. He was a cambion—half-human—like herself, but his other side, the Pollus, were distant cousins to Incubi. It made sense he looked almost as tasty as her cereal. But she wasn't attracted to him like *that*, which sometimes made her wonder if there was something wrong with her libido.

She couldn't do anything about it, anyway, so what was the point?

"Gross," Metcalf groaned. "Go do your preliminary mating stuff elsewhere."

"Preliminary mat—" Sylvester choked on his grape, coughing loudly enough to wake the dead.

Peony slapped him on the back, right between his shoulder blades, and the grape went flying.

"There goes my fruit intake for the day," Sylvester said sadly, his eyes watering a little.

She shook her head. "There's more fruit."

"Oh, I couldn't deprive the others."

"Such altruism," she said dryly.

"It's my middle name."

"Your middle name is 'disgusting'," Metcalf said. "How do you expect to be respected as a killer if you go around doing mating-stuff with the *doctor*?"

"It's flirting, Met. I'm not proposing to her." He flicked her an apologetic glance. "No offense."

"None taken."

"Then why do it?" The imp really did appear confused.

"I like my face to stay pretty. If she likes me, the next time I come in to get patched up, I walk away still pretty. Plus, it's fun."

His honesty was refreshing. While she got along—now—with most of the guild members, she knew they didn't all think of her as a friend. Couldn't, because the majority of the guild's members were slaves, with no control over their future. They had to be selfish to survive.

"That's the thing with you human-looking demons. You don't get true beauty." Metcalf cracked open a bone and sucked the marrow out. She fought the urge to gag.

Marrow should only be extracted for tests.

"Metcalf, you have a face only a mother could love."

"Eh, she didn't love me. Sold me into slavery." He smacked his thin lips together, black eyes watchful. "But I know real beauty when I see it."

"Be sure to let me know when you do," Sylvester said.

"I do, every day, in the mirror." And then Metcalf *winked*.

Sylvester laughed, and Peony bit her lip to keep from smiling. "It's the nose," she said. "It's totally the nose."

Metcalf nodded, his own small smile visible fleetingly.

When she'd first come to the guild, Metcalf had wanted to see what cambion tasted like, since he hadn't been able to take a bite out of Sylvester or Dru. He'd had her cornered, and she had been worried that she might kill him by accident, when Dru found them. Her sister had proceeded to beat the imp bloody, then shook him until his head wobbled for being such an idiot.

Taking a bite out of Peony would have left her in agony...and him dead.

After, Peony had offered to set the imp's nose, because, well, that's what she did. But Metcalf had wanted it to look broken, so she'd set it in a way that hadn't interfered with his sense of smell or breathing, but had given him a rather impressive bump.

He'd befriended her as a result.

And since Metcalf was one screw short of full-blown psychotic, the others had decided to leave the medic alone. Plus, she'd patched most of them up by now, so they tended to be grateful to her, rather than scared, like they were of Dru.

She fished out the last—soggy—Fruit Loop and shut her eyes as the sugary goodness exploded on her tongue. Would it be a bad thing if she drank the milk straight from the bowl? Deciding that she should save it for later, she turned her attention to the fruit and yogurt.

Sylvester's low murmur caught her attention. "Hey Doc, looks like the boss wants to talk to you."

Trick stood in the doorway to the mess, a finger pointed at her.

Someone had clearly never taught the blond demon manners.

"Right." She picked up the remains of her breakfast and gave the sweet milk a sad look.

"I'll clean it up for you," Sylvester said.

"Thanks."

She ate as she walked, and was briefly stopped by Germaine, one of the cooks. "Hey, Doc! Is Devi going to be okay?"

Devi was the Brevine demon she'd been treating before the angel had arrived. "She should be. I'll check on her soon."

Damn, I should have asked Sylvester how she was. He'd been put on nurse duty, because his Pollus half had healing abilities.

"Tell her I said 'hi'."

"Will do."

She passed on a few more greetings before reaching Trick. He glowered at her.

"Running late?" he asked.

"Didn't know I had an appointment." She shoveled in a mouthful of peaches and yogurt, so she couldn't make any more ire-inducing comments.

He spun on his heel. "Come with me."

CHAPTER 7

Zadkiel—no, Z—wanted to kill the yellow-haired demon. But alas, since his hands were tied and his body weak, there wasn't much he could do. One day he'd get free—provided he survived their 'medical treatment'—and then he'd seek his revenge.

They would all die.

Horribly.

And then he would hunt down the Infernus.

The screeching of metal against stone indicated that someone was entering the room, but he had no energy to lift his head.

"I'm back." That smooth masculine voice filled the small expanse.

Lucky me.

But he didn't bother replying. He couldn't, even if he'd wanted to.

Something rattled and clanged, and then the scent of sugar hit him. He inhaled deeply, enjoying how the aroma filled him, made him feel a little more alive. He didn't wonder too much why that was, but surely something so delicious would inspire anyone: angel, demon or human?

"Why are his hands tied up?" The feminine voice lashed across the room.

"He tried to rip his drip out."

"Then why is he gagged?"

"Tried to bite it out after that."

Z opened his eyes and took in the scene before him: Trick standing near the door, his golden hair mussed and annoyance draping his expression; the female demon with her hair braided, and her gloved hands on her hips; the medical cart with the torture supplies barely a yard from his prone form.

Can I kick it over?

Stupid question. He couldn't even get up to urinate.

The thought made red flood his cheeks and his eyes close. Trick had been required to help him last night, and it had been beyond embarrassing. It just showed how pathetic he'd become.

Surely they won't let me back into Heaven after this.

He could only hope they ignored his transgressions. Angelic warriors did not get captured, and they did not have their wings plucked, nor did they have demons help them vacate their bladders.

For some reason, it was the latter that infuriated him the most at present.

"Did you explain to him why he had the drip?"

"He wasn't exactly rational."

Oh, he was very rational. He had to escape, and they were pumping poison into his body. Why else would he not heal?

"I'll check him over." She exchanged her red gloves

for plastic ones.

"You do that."

"Have you gotten a report from Sylvester about Devi?" she asked as she rummaged around on the trolley.

"You were eating breakfast with him, why didn't you ask?"

"Because I was eating breakfast."

Trick rolled his eyes. "She'll live. Although, once I'm through with her, she'll probably wish she hadn't survived. Robbing from an assassin—and getting caught—just highlights her stupidity."

Then the male demon left, leaving Z alone with the female and her torture plans.

She placed some kind of device around her neck, then stepped closer to him. "If I remove the gag, will you promise to behave?"

He wanted to do no such thing, but there was a kindness in her gaze that he couldn't ignore; no matter that she had caused him so much agony he'd passed out previously.

Did she do it on purpose? Or had she been trying to help?

It was something he'd been wondering ever since.

Eventually, he nodded.

A small zap of magic lanced through his muscles, causing him to tense.

"I'll be careful," she said, misreading his body language.

Foolish. He'd forgotten that promising something to a demon would bind him. At least it was to the female, and not Trick.

The gag was gone. He took a deep breath, then coughed, his mouth and throat as dry as desert sands.

"Here." She held out a cup of water with a straw. "Sip it slowly."

He complied, mostly because he knew if he gulped the liquid, he'd choke.

"There. Now why did you try and take out the drip?"

He shut his eyes, so he didn't have to see the earnest concern in her gaze. *It's all a lie.*

Gentle fingers on his arm, near where the needle pierced his skin. She tutted. "You've done some damage. I am going to have to remove this and do it again."

"No."

Had he spoken? Or had it just screamed it in his head?

But her hands touched his face, forcing him to open his eyes. "'No' what?"

"I don't want your poison."

There, he'd said it. Admitted he knew what she was doing.

"Poison?" A frown marred the smooth golden skin of her forehead.

"From the bag." He nodded at the clear plastic sack hanging from some kind of metal coat hook.

She examined the withered bag. "This is saline, a salt-water fluid to help rehydrate you."

"I am sickening." He hadn't wanted to admit that, but it was clear.

"Not from the fluid. You were ill before you came here."

That was true. But if they kept him weak...

He wouldn't be controlled. Not by demons.

"I promise it's saline. Here." She went to a new bag and attached a plastic tube to it. She then pooled some of the liquid into his cup and handed him the straw. "Drink it."

He stared at her, trying to see the deception, but her gaze was clear, and her voice spoke nothing but truth. He took a sip and winced. Salt water.

He tilted his chin down. "I should be healing."

She set the cup on the trolley then squatted, so they were eye-level. "Your wings have been plucked, you have a fractured skull, potential broken spine, they harvested some of your organs and that's just the things I know about."

All things he should have healed from, but the broken spine and skull could take time because of his young age.

"How long have I been injured?"

She shook her head. "I don't know."

Truth.

She waited for him to say more, but he just shut his eyes again. He was tired. Tired of feeling pain, tired of knowing he was a failure. And he hated the compassion in her clear gray gaze: like she could see his discomfort and would have taken it from him, if she could.

She began doing things to his wings, moving the useless appendages in different directions, dabbing coldness over the skeletal limbs. Stinging followed the dabbing, but it was nothing like the previous evening.

Then she pressed a cold disc to his back and stood next to his prone form, her body heat warming his left side. The scent of sugar increased. Eventually, her hands worked over him from head to toe, her touch professional and dispassionate.

"Okay."

He opened his eyes. She was squatting next to him again.

"You're no different to yesterday, although I do agree with your theory that you've been poisoned. You're covered in bruises from my touch, which indicates internal bleeding. You have a loss of muscle tension, your blood pressure is low today—but I don't know what's normal for an angel—and your nailbeds are purple. Not the classic signs of poisoning in humans, but all things that shouldn't really be happening to an immortal."

He couldn't stop the question from emerging. "How do you know what happens to a human?"

Had she gone around poisoning humans before coming to work for the guild? It would make sense.

She rocked back, her mouth pinching. "I was a doctor."

Was.

She'd been a *healer* before coming to an assassin guild? There was a mystery there, one he decided he didn't want to solve. He was better off knowing nothing about her, because when the Darts came for him, she'd die along with everyone else.

Heaven's army had no compassion for demons.

"A demon doctor," he muttered, deliberately trying to cause distance between them. To destroy this sense of her decency. "Try a different lie next time."

Her expression grew shuttered and she stood.

He wanted to warn her, to make her fear him, even though he was weak and prone. "When my friends come for me—and they will—you will die along with the rest of them. Demons don't help people. And angels kill demons."

She ignored his warning, her bearing calm and purposeful. "Hopefully the saline will flush some of the toxin from your system." Then she took the drip and inserted a new one.

It hurt.

And from the look on her face, it had been meant to.

CHAPTER 8

The angel had barely spoken to her in three weeks.

Peony shouldn't have been annoyed by his silence—it sure was better than the eternal complaining some of her human patients had enjoyed—but he wouldn't even answer questions that would help her treat him. It was as if he honestly believed she was trying to harm him *more*.

I am a doctor, damnit.

Not that he believed her.

No, she was a demon who couldn't possibly be a healer, and his friends would kill her. That was about the sum of their conversation to date, and it infuriated her that he thought so little of her.

It shouldn't matter.

No, it really shouldn't.

Then why do you keep dreaming about him?

That, she'd prefer not to think about.

Developing a crush on a patient was disgusting, and she preferred not to think of herself in those terms.

Frowning, she typed her latest observations and notes into the computer she'd forced Trick to buy for the clinic.

The single-room space was a bit cluttered, but she liked it. She'd managed to cram a gurney, desk and supplies cabinet into the room, and even had a small defibrillator mounted on a wall. Not that she was sure she could use it on most demons, since they seemed to all have different heartrates, but she was in the process of convincing one of the more IT-savvy assassins to help her try and re-program the thing. She should follow up with Merrick later.

She finished her notes and then signed out of the medical program. Peony shared the MacBook Air with Sylvester, her reluctant conscripted nurse, and she couldn't risk him seeing the client record, although, this particular file *was* password-protected: he'd never see its contents. Sylvester, however, was one of their best thieves—the man defined sneaky.

Trick still wanted the angel kept a secret, at least the angel's skull was healed.

Three weeks, and it was no longer the spongy mess she'd first felt. Solid bone under warm skin had greeted her today, and she'd done a little happy dance when she'd gotten back to her clinic. It meant that whatever poison had been given to the angel—and was still affecting him—was no longer hampering his healing ability.

Hopefully that meant his wings would grow back soon, but he had a long way to go to heal fully. He was still emaciated, and she wasn't certain his organs had entirely re-formed, since the whites of his eyes were stained a faint yellow. She'd overheard Metcalf saying a week ago that angel liver was considered a delicacy, along with human toes, Envio horns and other things she'd prefer to forget.

Human toes, though?

Lucky for her he'd decided she was inedible, otherwise she'd have to invest in steel-capped shoes.

She checked her inbox, sent a short reply to an email from her mother, then closed the laptop. Selene liked to check in on Peony daily, and while it was a little overbearing, she understood her mother's fears. Peony had practically been raised as a human, and it was only when she'd hit puberty that things had gone...badly. When she'd realized that her dreams were just that: dreams.

She'd gone from being a normal kid to covering almost every inch of bare skin overnight and cowering away from people. It was amazing how lonely you could be, surrounded by smiling and laughing faces, but when your skin was toxic to the touch, you didn't have room for mistakes. And being friends with a human was just that: a mistake.

So she'd cut her friends from her life. The other girls had been hurt—and had turned cruel, as a result—but they wouldn't have been able to understand that Peony wasn't like them, that she couldn't even risk an accidental touch. There were no potential make-up trials or hair-dying shenanigans, no hugs or cheek-kisses in her future.

Instead she'd focused on her studies. She hadn't been willing to give up on becoming a doctor, too.

The door to the room burst open, startling her.

"Trick."

Her boss stood on the threshold, his eyes narrowed and his expression thunderous. She had no idea what had caused his irritation, but she hoped he wouldn't take it out on her.

He shut the door behind him, then flicked his fingers. The room popped with electricity: he'd established a ward or anti-listening spell of some kind. She didn't bother standing.

"How is the angel?"

"He's responding well to treatment," Peony replied. Physically, at least.

Trick stared at her, his brown eyes hard. "Cut his wings off."

Peony flinched. "I don't think that's necessary—"

"They will be hindering his recovery. He is no good to me weak and injured."

"But he's starting to heal."

"His wings are no better."

"No, but his skull fracture has healed completely, at least, as far as I can tell. I think that his body is now repairing the most vital injuries first."

He stared at her.

She placed her hands on her knees. "I think whatever poison they gave him, it hindered his healing abilities." Trick opened his mouth, but she rushed to keep talking. "I don't know of a substance that could do that to angels, but whatever it is, the angel seems to be recovering from it. And he's starting to heal on his own."

Please don't take his wings.

Images swamped her, of the angel being strapped down while a scalpel, followed by a bone saw, brutally cut his wings away. Horror seized her, her heartbeat accelerating. She didn't know where the thought came from, but she knew that taking his wings would break this injured angel, maybe irreparably, and she couldn't be part of that. Didn't want to see it, didn't want to allow it.

Trick sighed. "We can't afford to keep him locked in that cell indefinitely. It will be bad for his psychological health, and I need him able to function."

She sat back and crossed her arms over her chest. "If you cut his wings off, it will cause more damage than keeping him in that room."

"They'll grow back." He shrugged. "Eventually."

"Can you be sure? He isn't recovering normally."

He took a while to reply. "No, I can't be sure."

"He won't be any good without his wings." They were part of who he was. Just like her damned skin had become an essential part of her.

He didn't look convinced. "Angels can survive without wings."

She'd heard the rumors. "Fallen ones."

Trick opened his mouth, but shut it with a snap when the door slammed into his back. He pivoted on the balls of his feet and called out to whoever was trying to come in. "What?"

"We need the doctor, sir," a voice squeaked from behind the door. "Opal is hurt bad."

Peony stood. "What happened? Where is she?"

"Here!"

She shoved her chair back to the desk and then got her supplies ready. "Trick, move out of the way."

He sidled from the door, and two demons pushed through, dragging a limp form between them. They hauled Opal onto the gurney, and then backed away. "She's heavier than she looks."

Peony flicked them a glance, then hurried to Opal's side. The Radiato demon's clothing was stiff, and hard to work around.

"She's heavy," Trick said, "because her clothing is lead-lined."

Opal's beige skin was ashen, and she was mumbling under her breath. Purple blood was oozing from the seams of her clothing. Peony peeled back the cloth, but a firm grip on her fabric-covered wrist made her pause.

Trick spoke in a low, intense tone. "Be careful how much clothing you remove."

"I need to assess her wounds."

"She's out of her mind and she's a Radiato. She could fry everyone with radiation."

"They mostly use X-rays—"

"Which are deadly in high doses."

"I know that, but the amount of exposure—"

"Radiato are deadly. There's a reason you don't see them much. And when they are in distress they can produce gamma and neutron radiation as well."

She stared at him for a moment.

Damnit.

She turned back to her patient, but struggled to find where the blood was coming from. She peeled back more and more layers of lead-lined cloth, finally finding a knife wound on her ribs. Air bubbled at the site, blood pouring out.

She grabbed her stethoscope and listened intently to Opal's lungs.

Traumatic pneumothorax.

Chest tube insertion was the best option.

She got to work, pulling the clothing away and getting her supplies ready.

"Everyone, leave the room," Trick ordered. To Peony,

he said, "I'm not putting the others at risk."

She flicked him a glance. *Oh, so it's okay if I die.*

But he remained.

Tuning the demon out, she carefully inserted some plastic tubing though a small incision she'd made. A wave of energy burst from Opal, searing the side of Peony's face and hands. She gasped as her latex gloves melted, and her cheek burned red hot. Nausea and dizziness hit her hard, and she gagged, hunching over. Wrenching away, she tore off the gloves, peeling skin in the process. She clenched her teeth against the pain.

"What the Hell—?"

She ignored Trick's surprise. Instead, with hands that shook and oozed, she pulled as much of Opal's clothing back over her as she could, using extreme care so that her skin did not come into contact with any of the Radiato's exposed flesh.

"I need you to pack the wound."

She spun away, somehow managing to find a seat. She wheeled the desk chair over to the pharmaceutical cabinet and sink, pausing as the room careened around her. Once she could think past the dizziness, she washed her hands in cold water, hissing at the pain. She flinched as the skin sloughed off her hands, but it didn't leave exposed tissue; instead pink, raw new skin was apparent.

Thank the gods for my healing abilities.

Even though Peony and Dru were identical twins, Peony's ability to heal surpassed her sister's, and pretty much every other demon she knew.

Wondering how she was going to get her face under the tap, she grabbed some paper towel, soaked it, and then dabbed it against her burned cheek. Skin came away with the towel, but she chose not to worry about it. After all, if her hands were healing already, her face would be too.

What next?

She turned to make sure Trick had packed the wound, and saw he was placing gauze over the cut and tubing. It would have to do for now. Opal moaned, her head thrashing. Trick quickly shoved the lead-lined clothing back in place and jumped away. Another burst of energy shot through the room, although neither one of them was in the line of fire this time.

"I'm going to have to check everyone for radiation poisoning, aren't I?" she asked.

Trick nodded.

Then, for the first time, his brown eyes looked at her with something almost like...concern. "Are you going to be okay?"

"Probably."

She seriously doubted he cared about her; he was no doubt concerned about Dru's reaction. If Peony died and Trick had been around to prevent it...

Antibiotics, she thought. Even though she was healing quickly, she couldn't see what internal damage had been done. Bone marrow was often compromised in acute cases, and since her burns had come up almost instantaneously, she assumed that would be the case for her. If she was purely human, she'd be dead within twenty-four to forty-eight hours.

Thanks, Dad.

For once, her Mortus genes weren't a hindrance.

"What about you?" she asked, after swallowing a horse-sized tablet antibiotic.

"I will be fine."

She had no idea what kind of demon he was, but she assumed he knew his species' limits.

"Don't want me to check you out, just in case?"

"I'd prefer not."

She shrugged, then grimaced; that had not helped her nausea. Then again, the giant pill probably hadn't, either. She should have taken it with food.

"I really need to check her for more injuries," Peony said. But she didn't want to put new gloves on, and she was suddenly so tired, holding her head up was an effort.

"I'll get Sylvester," Trick said. "He can check you out and give you some extra juice if you need it."

"Okay."

She didn't like relying on Sylvester's healing ability, because it felt like cheating. All it took was a single touch, and he knew what was wrong with someone and how to heal them. It didn't mean he *could* heal them every time; some things were beyond magic. But it gave him an unfair advantage, and one he didn't particularly like.

He was a thief, not a doctor, so he liked to tell her.

She would have given her left arm to have his powers. Then again, she probably wouldn't have been able to use them.

Her touch, after all, was deadly.

CHAPTER 9

Z was screaming, yet no one heard him.

Not that he was screaming aloud, but telepathically, and only at the other Darts. Still there was no reply, nothing but a gray mist that absorbed the sound of his cries.

Is it a result of the brain injury?

It was possible, he supposed.

Dina or Raziel would know, but they weren't answering.

He shut his eyes, pressing his face down on his forearms as he tried to remember more details about the attack on Heaven. There was little left in his memory: patrolling as normal, then being attacked by the Infernus and his falling to the ground. Dina's unknown fate gnawed at him. Was she captured, too? Had she escaped?

He would have thought that the other Darts would have come for him by now, and that they hadn't worried him. Perhaps they had given up on him for being the utter failure that he was. Or had they been captured, too, when they had come to assist in the fight?

And what happened to Heaven's Heart?

Surely it hadn't been taken. God wouldn't have allowed it, no matter that he only spoke through the archangels. His will was law.

Raising a hand, he touched the back of his skull. Firm bone and the rough stubble of new hair met his questing fingers. He'd been skeptical about the female demon's assistance, but there was no denying his headaches had eased, and he wasn't feeling like death hovered on the horizon. He still didn't feel well, though. Pain was a constant companion, and his wings were a shredded mess of bone and tissue. At least he was no longer paralyzed, just weak.

Very weak.

He was more comfortable lying on the stone floor of his cell than the bed, and crawled there at the first opportunity he had. It meant he could also spread his wings out a little, easing the ache that resulted from keeping them confined. Whenever the healer found him though, she would pick him up and place him back on the bed. He hadn't told her it hurt more to lie there, mostly because he'd been trying to avoid speaking to her at all.

He didn't want to see her empathy, didn't want to feel her pity. And he didn't want to hear her voice.

She still spoke to him, though.

Asking him questions about how his wounded body felt, wanting to know about this, prodding that. He'd never really had much to do with healers, and had to wonder if his treatment was typical.

He'd probably never find out.

He was an angel in a demon den. If he made it out of

here alive, it was unlikely he'd need such medical intervention again. Because once he was gone, he'd kill Trick, go after the Infernus, and if he survived all that, then he'd fight his way back into Heaven. If they wouldn't have him, well, he'd be better off dead.

The metallic screech of the door opening dragged him away from his degenerating thoughts. The healer backed into the room, her long white hair tied back in its normal braid.

"I'm fine," she grumbled at someone outside.

"Trick wants me to assist."

"Just...don't hover over me."

An affronted snort. "I don't hover. I loom menacingly."

The supply trolley rattled inside the cell and a man followed. It wasn't Trick.

Another demon.

Z shouldn't have been surprised. He was in a demon assassin guild, after all.

This one looked human, with brown hair and a fighter's physique. Z wouldn't be surprised if he was handy with knives and smiled while using them on someone.

A low whistle pierced the air. "Is that what I think it is?"

The female healer spun around and spotted Z lying on the floor. Her expression turned pinched. "Yes. And you should say 'he' not 'it'."

She was offended on his behalf.

Z's eyes locked on the bandages on her hands and the ruined skin on one side of her face. *What happened?* The words almost burst from him without his consent. Her normally healthy golden skin was wan, and she looked like she'd been tortured. He *had* to know who had hurt her. He would make whoever did it pay.

No, you won't. You are going to kill her boss and let her live. That will be your thanks for her care.

But right now, the slight flicker of pain in her gaze had all his protective instincts raging. And here he was, prone on the stone floor in a cell and practically useless. He shook his head. He was an idiot.

"Doc, that's an angel. They may have the right kind of tackle, but they don't use it. Angels aren't *men*. Or women, for that matter. They just are. Using the right pronoun isn't a big deal."

"Tackle?" She turned to look at the demon and winced at the movement. He didn't like to see her in discomfort, and that worried him. Why should he even care? She was a demon.

But she's unlike any demon you've met before.

"You know, genitalia."

Z blinked. They were talking about his...private parts?

She flushed a little. "Sylvester—"

"Incubus," Z said suddenly.

Both demons turned to stare at him.

"If you're thinking of my...penis in preference to anything else, you must be some kind of Incubus." Most other demons would view him as a threat first, something worth eating or something worth selling, second. Not whether or not he could reproduce.

A dark eyebrow arched. "Distantly related."

The healer licked her cracked lower lip. "I thought the Pollus were part Incubus."

The demon waved a hand. "Cousins. Of a sort."

Z could tell the demon was telling the truth, although it wasn't the *entire* truth.

This was all lovely, but it didn't explain why the healer's hands were bandaged and her face looked like she'd been burned.

He didn't ask.

That would display his interest, and he'd spent the past few weeks clearly indicating that he didn't care about anything other than his upcoming rescue.

The healer seemed to have decided that line of conversation was at an end. "Can you do the checkup today?"

"Sure thing, Doc." Sylvester directed a careless smile at her. Z clenched his jaw.

The male demon approached him and squatted down. "You try anything aggressive, angel-boy, and I won't play nice."

Truth.

"Sylvester!"

Z met the demon's blue stare. "I am in no condition to do you harm. Otherwise, I already would have."

The healer turned shocked eyes on him.

Z would have shrugged, but he was lying flat on his stomach and his back was a mess of pain.

"You would have *tried* to harm me. You wouldn't have succeeded," the Pollus demon said.

That was absurd. Z was a fully-fledged angel—most demons wouldn't stand a chance against him, not if he was at full strength, anyway. The man didn't seem entirely purebred, however. Maybe it gave him an edge.

"Want my stethoscope?" the healer asked.

"Don't need it." The demon then clasped Z's wrist in

a strong grip, and a strange magic raced through his limbs. He tried to pull away, but the demon was sturdy and held on.

Demon magic is in *me.*

Panic swirled through his mind, and his heart rate increased. Then, suddenly, the demon let go. Z pulled his arm back, staring at his wrist as if it had betrayed him.

"He's stable. I gave him some extra juice to help him heal, so you might see an improvement in a day or two."

Excitement lit the female's eyes. "We could—"

"I know what you're thinking, and no. He fought me. And he probably will again. Plus, demon energy may not be good long-term for an angel. Short-term, it will help him heal the main injuries, like the half-missing liver."

The assassin demon was a natural born healer?

Z's mind spun. There weren't many angel healers, and they were highly prized. With red-gold filaments in their wings, they were trained from the moment they showed their first metallic thread.

Now, he'd met two demons who both could heal. One through magic and one through learning.

What else don't I know?

A low buzzing sound filled the room. "Shit." The Pollus demon fished a phone from his back pocket. "I need to take this." He disappeared through the door.

The healer squatted next to Z. "You should be on the bed."

He shook his head.

"I can't check your vitals today, but I assume Sylvester is happy. I should be able to, tomorrow." Her gaze turned vacant. "I wish he'd take blood pressure, at least. Ah well."

"What happened?" By the skies, he hadn't meant to ask, but without intending to, Z's hand rose to touch her uninjured cheek. He was a bare inch away when, whip-fast, she knocked his limb away.

Her voice was low, earnest, and stern. "Don't ever touch me."

"I—"

"Never touch my skin."

Sylvester called through the doorway. "Yo, Doc, I gotta go. Let's wrap this up."

Without looking at Z, she rose to her feet and then pushed the trolley out the room with her forearms. She didn't look back.

Z found himself wishing she had.

CHAPTER 10

Peony frowned at the knock on her bedroom door. It was past midnight and she should be asleep, what with the radiation burns and her body working overtime to repair the damage, but she couldn't stop picturing the angel's face when she'd knocked his hand away.

Confusion. Hurt. Shock.

It was the first time he'd tried to touch her—to reach out in any way to her—and she'd rebuffed him. How was she going to gain his trust if he thought that she was rejecting him at the first chance she got?

The knocking continued.

Sighing, she got up, headed to the door and opened it a crack. Sylvester stood on the other side, his black jeans and leather jacket speckled with raindrops.

"Can I come in?"

He'd never come to her room before—she hadn't even known he knew where it was.

"Sure." She stepped back.

He strode inside and gave the chamber a very quick, but no doubt thorough, assessment. His gaze settled on the book left on her wrinkled bedspread.

"Harry Potter?" His chestnut eyebrow rose.

"What? It's a classic."

"When people say classic, I think of *The Epic of Gilgamesh, The Odyssey, A Christmas Carol, The Picture of Dorian Gray, Pride and Prejudice*."

Peony chuckled. "How old are you, exactly?"

"None of your damned business." He crossed his arms over his broad chest, and leaned against a wall. He smelled of pine trees and fresh rain.

She sat on the end of her bed. "To what do I owe this visit?"

Even though the cambion might flirt with her over meals, she knew his coming here wasn't about sex. Not only was she totally off limits—all the demons here knew that—he had never shown any real interest in her.

Maybe he's checking up on me?

The skin on her hands was still a raw pink, but she could move them without pain, and her cheek was in much the same condition. Slightly better, really, since she hadn't ripped off bits of her flesh from her face, as she had when she'd pulled away the melted gloves.

Sylvester grabbed something from his pocket and then walked to each corner of her room, sprinkling what looked like glitter into the four corners. *Great. That's going to never go away.* She'd be finding glitter on her stuff for months, years, even.

He then barked a word under his breath, and the room sizzled briefly with magic.

Anti-listening spell.

She met his gaze. "That serious, huh?"

"Peony, this is some bad shit." He pulled up a chair

and sat.

"The burns? They're healing."

"Don't play dumb. The angel."

"He's injured, he can't do anything to hurt me."

Sylvester shook his head. "I know Trick reckons he's made a good deal, but that's a real live fucking angel in our building. If he has buddies who are going to come for him, we're all screwed."

"He keeps saying they will, but no one has shown up yet."

"I assume that's cos Trick has warded the shit out of the room. It doesn't mean they won't come, especially after the angel gets his strength back."

"And what am I meant to do about it?" she asked.

Something hard gleamed in Sylvester's normally amused gaze. "Kill the angel and be done with it."

She rocked back with shock. "What? *No.*"

"Angels and demons don't mix. Even if Trick manages to keep this guy as a slave, the instant he's free, he will come back for us. You and Trick especially."

Something like despair swirled through her. "But I've been *helping* him."

"He may not see it that way."

She jutted her chin out. "I'll make him see reason."

"Even if he spares you, what about the others?"

"He'll get to know us—"

"Don't play dumb."

"It's not like I have a choice in this. Trick wants me to heal, I heal. If you have an issue, take it up with Trick."

"Oh, I did. All he sees is the potential paycheck in his future."

"I'm not going to kill my patient." Every instinct in her

rejected the idea, not withstanding her own promise.

"Fine. Tell Dru."

She frowned. "Tell Dru what?"

"Tell her about the angel. See what she can do."

"I don't see what she could do that we can't. And I'm not going to stand by and watch her kill him, either."

Sylvester stood. "Trick really wants to try and get into your sister's pants, even though everyone knows that's signing his own death warrant. His lust might make him listen to her."

"I'm not allowed to tell anyone, or I'm dead."

"He didn't tell me that rule." A casual shrug. "So she might have heard it from me."

"I see."

"You tell her, or I will. And you can imagine the decision she'll make if I am the one who passes the info on."

Dru would find the angel and kill him. She'd apologize to Trick after, deepen her debt, but she'd do it. Dru's self-focus would work against Peony here: her twin knew that if the guild failed, she'd go down with it. And having an angel prisoner...

"I'll talk to her," Peony said.

Sylvester strode to the door. "Good. Do it soon. I will talk to Trick again tomorrow."

Then he was gone, and the angel's life hung in the balance.

Again.

Dru stumbled to a halt in her room, failing to notice Peony waiting. Her sister was wearing a form-fitting black dress, and her white hair was out and spilled over her shoulders. *She was on a job*, Peony realized. Dru didn't dress like that normally—she was a loose jeans, T-shirt and weapons kind of woman. Anything that allowed her free movement was a good choice, and anything that hid weapons was an ever better one.

Peony had let herself into Dru's room, using the spare key her sister had given her as a sort of peace offering. She'd never used it before, preferring to visit when something had been prearranged, but she didn't trust that Sylvester wouldn't corner Dru the first chance he had, and so she'd taken advantage of the small piece of trust Dru had given her.

Her twin sister's room was one of the biggest in the guild, and it was fitted out nicely, with a large bed, walk-in-robe and its own private bathroom. Dru had good taste in furniture, and everything was elegant and streamlined.

Must be nice to have the boss pine after you.

It was funny, while Dru and Peony shared the same face, Trick had never once looked at her with anything approaching attraction. Dru didn't seem to care that Trick had a crush on her; she acted like his infatuation didn't even exist.

She still hadn't noticed Peony's presence.

"Dru!"

No reply, just a wild-eyed stare. Had something happened to her? Where had she been? *Maybe I should have brought my gear...*

Peony carefully rubbed her palms together. She was

wearing gloves to hide her hands, and her cheek just looked like she'd had some really hardcore exfoliation on one side, but she hoped her sister didn't notice she'd been injured. Dru's brand of concern often left someone dead, and poor Opal hadn't hurt her deliberately.

Still no acknowledgement from her sister.

"Dru, you're back."

Her twin strode further into the room and sat on the edge of her bed. She kicked off her high heels, a loud sigh bursting forth as she wriggled her toes. "What's wrong?"

No 'hello', no 'how are you?', just a 'what's wrong?'. It was so utterly Dru. She was a problem solver, and to her, there was always a problem.

Peony bit her lip. "I don't like my latest assignment."

Wow, that had come out more whiny that she'd anticipated.

"Peony—" There was a warning in her sister's voice, like her patience was limited and she did not have time for Peony's antics.

The thing was, Peony didn't *have* antics. And she wasn't trying to back out of the job because it was too hard. Sure, she'd failed her first few assignments, when Trick had wanted to her to thieve or kill, but since she'd been given her clinic, she'd done almost everything he'd asked.

But she knew Dru, and she knew what her sister was thinking.

"No, it's not that I'm too soft." She slashed a trembling hand through the air. Shit. Her body was still suffering from Opal's radiation. She'd have to make this quick, before she passed out and Dru realized something was really wrong. "Dru, this is dangerous. And *wrong*."

"All right." Dru frowned. "Why is it wrong?"

How to phrase this? Peony glanced around the room, hoping for some inspiration. She knew Dru would have warded this space against listening spells, so it was safe to talk...but it was her life on the line. Hers and the angel's. She couldn't stuff this up.

"Peony?"

Peony stepped forward, until she was so close to Dru that she caught the scent of sandalwood.

Why did her sister smell like a man's cologne?

"He has an angel here," she whispered.

"*What*?" Dru jumped to her feet so fast Peony didn't have a chance to dodge out of the way. She lost her balance—damn radiation sickness—and toppled to the floor. The tie on her hair gave way, and loose strands flew out over her face. Her palms stung as they hit the ground and her butt protested.

"Thanks," Peony muttered.

Just what she'd needed.

"Ooops." Dru reached out a hand and hauled Peony to her feet, careful to grip her sleeve. Even though they were twins, Dru didn't take the risk of skin-to-skin contact, and she avoided Peony's hands, as if they were more toxic than the rest of her.

"He has a...a...." Dru couldn't even say the word.

Peony brushed herself off, but kept her gaze locked on the ground. She didn't want to see Dru's expression. Things were bad if she couldn't even say 'angel'. "It's not right," she murmured.

"No, it's not." Dru balled her hand into a fist. "It's too dangerous." There was an ominous pause. "How did Trick get an angel?"

Peony flinched at the anger simmering in her sister's words, but she had to keep her oath to Trick—to keep the deal with the Infernus secret. No matter what, though, she couldn't let Dru hurt the angel. "He's sick."

"Trick? You got that right."

Wait, what?

"Not Trick. The angel."

"I'm not following," Dru said. "Start at the beginning."

Peony swallowed. "About a month ago,"— three weeks, but she didn't need to be that specific—"Trick showed me his new...recruit. The angel. And he was sick, like really sick. Poisoned with something, I don't know what. But it seems magical in origin, maybe demonic, I don't know. I've been looking after him as my latest 'assignment'." She made finger quotes around the last word.

"Is it dying?" Dru asked. "Does it still have...*wings*?"

Peony grimaced. "Yes to the wings, and probably to the dying."

He seemed to have improved, but he was still suffering from the poison. If his body never learned to fight it off, he'd die eventually. She would have to find a cure, not that she had the resources to do it.

"Has it tried to attack you?"

Peony shook her head. She had to be honest. "No. But he says his friends will come for him. And I believe him. They will kill whoever they can to get to him, that I don't doubt."

Why did everyone refer to the angel as 'it'? He was a living being, and he seemed so very male, even in his current state. When he was well, she knew he'd be overpoweringly masculine.

I didn't just think that.

"Those wings must be worth a fortune," Dru muttered.

Peony recalled the angel as she'd first seen him and rage poured through her. "No feathers are left. They're all but destroyed from whatever poison he was given."

Dru shut her eyes for a few seconds, thinking. "So, what do you want me to do about it?"

"Help me?" She hadn't meant for it to sound so pathetic. And she hadn't mentioned Sylvester's threat at all, yet. But she didn't want to give Dru the idea that killing the angel was their best option—not if that idea hadn't already occurred to her.

Death didn't mean much to an assassin.

"This kind of job would be top secret. How am I going to approach Trick about it? It could mean you get hurt."

"You could find the angel on your own? Then say something about your discovery."

Dru gave her a skeptical glance. "And how easy would that be?"

Peony thought about the secret corridor in Trick's office. "Not easy."

"I'll see what I can do without risking your life."

Peony reached out a gloved hand, let it hover over Dru's shoulder but not touching, knowing her sister preferred it that way. "Thank you."

There, she'd done it. At least she could tell Sylvester that Dru was onto it.

But her sister shook her head. "Don't thank me yet."

Great.

CHAPTER 11

The demon healer looked better today. Her hands were no longer bandaged but gloved, like normal, and the skin on her face was fresh and shiny and glowing with health. Z wanted to feel if it was as soft as it looked.

You only want to touch her because she said you couldn't.

Yes, that was it.

It wasn't that she was quite pretty, or that he had grown to love watching the emotions that flickered behind her steady gray gaze. No, it wasn't that, because he wasn't attracted to her. He was just suffering from Stockholm Syndrome or something like it. She was his captor as much as Trick was. He was just susceptible to her kindness, because he'd been denied it for so long.

But something about their encounter yesterday had changed the way he thought about her, and he wasn't going to pretend otherwise. Self-hatred soon followed— he had begun to long for the company of a creature he had once been sworn to kill on sight.

Was still probably sworn to kill.

"It's that time already?" he asked, then cursed himself.

"Will you help me lift you up?" Peony asked. He grunted a reply, not trusting himself to speak.

She took great care as she lifted him onto the pallet, gently folding his wings away to avoid any additional jostling. It still hurt, but he wasn't going to show her his pain, even though he could feel new bruises forming under his skin. He was beginning to crave her touch, just to feel another's warmth, to know he wasn't so alone.

She bit her lip as she stared at his marred skin.

"They're fine," he said, willing her to believe him. "The bruises. Don't worry about them."

"I'm your doctor, I have to worry about them."

"And whoever heard of a demon doctor before?" *There I go again with the rudeness.* Something within Z protested at their burgeoning closeness, and it instinctively struck out.

"I've been tending to you for weeks; I'm not going anywhere until you're well."

Truth.

"How did an angel get sold into demon slavery, anyway?" she asked. No sooner had she spoken than her eyes widened, like she was mortified.

Had she surprised herself with the question?

He snorted. "We weren't prepared and we got raided. I was taken. My friends will come get me. I've told you that."

That was the simple version. The only problem? The complicated version wasn't much longer, courtesy of his head wound and memory loss.

He knew beyond a doubt now, however, that he wouldn't leave her to die with Trick when the Darts came for him. No, he'd keep her safe.

Somehow.

"You told me the latter." She shrugged. "Everyone can have daydreams, I guess. But just remember, they're dreams. You're deep in Hell now." She wrapped a cuff around his arm and concentrated as she inflated it. Z had no idea what it was, but the information it provided seemed to mean a great deal to her.

She thinks my chances of freedom are a fantasy. Maybe she was right.

"What are your daydreams?" he asked, suddenly desperate to know the answer. To know more about *her.*

She paused. "I don't have any. Not anymore. There's no point."

Truth. Laced with sadness.

"I thought demons always wanted what they can't have," he murmured, trying to wipe the melancholy from her expression. *You could have been nicer in your attempt,* his conscience snapped.

No, I couldn't have.

"And I thought angels were smarmy jerks who thought they were better than everyone else."

Surprised, he chuckled at her tone. "Touché."

She put the stethoscope down and ripped the Velcro open on the cuff. As she rummaged around on her torture cart for something, she asked, "What's your name?"

He looked at the wall. "I don't have one anymore."

"Why not?"

"When I was taken, I lost my right to my wings."

"Is that why they're...dying?"

It was a valid theory, he supposed, but unlikely. He'd never heard of an angel—even a young one—losing their wings through such circumstances.

"No."

Silence descended on the cell while she waited for him to say more. When he didn't elaborate, she said, "You'll live for another day."

She cleaned up her equipment, then pushed the cart toward the door.

Ask. Just ask.

He hadn't wanted to reveal any more than he already had, but he needed to know. "Was there...another angel brought here with me?" He half-raised himself up on an elbow, watching her face intently. He would hear the lie, but he wanted—no, needed—to see her face as she replied.

Her mouth dropped open before she blurted, "Another *angel*?"

He nodded.

"No."

Truth.

Disappointment slammed through him.

Dina wasn't here. At least, not as far as the demon healer was aware. Trick could have bought Dina as well, but she would have to have been in far worse condition than Z to be held here with no one else the wiser. And the healer would have been involved, then.

He lay back down.

He was on his own.

Dina was out there, maybe captured, maybe free.

The Darts hadn't come looking for him.

Had they given up? Or had the Infernus covered their tracks too well?

The healer opened the door, the clanging jarring him from his thoughts.

"Z," he muttered, just before she stepped outside the cell.

"What?" She looked over her shoulder at him.

"Call me Z."

CHAPTER 12

"You're not healing as fast as I would like, but the tissue is starting to mend." Peony gently placed a clean gauze strip over Opal's wound, and then used waterproof tape to secure it.

The Radiato demon looked down at the bandage, then back up at Peony. "Thanks, Doc. And I really am sorry." The beige-skinned demon winced as she looked at Peony's healed cheek.

Peony ducked her head and spun her chair to face the desk, quickly typing some notes into her computer. "It's no problem."

Opal had been nothing but remorseful since she'd come to a couple days ago. It was embarrassing.

A thin arm entered her line of vision as Opal gripped her sleeve. She turned to face the Radiato demon, shocked that the other woman had initiated physical contact.

Opal's eyes were wide in her face, their irises a kaleidoscope of green and brown hues. "No, Doc, I mean it. Most healers wouldn't have come near a Radiato who was in my state. They would have left me to die. We were lucky you survived my emissions, sure. But you didn't know you would. So, I owe you one. For real."

There was nothing but sincerity in the demon's expression and voice.

Peony nodded. "I was just doing my job—what was *right*."

She wasn't doing it to earn favors.

Earn her freedom—sure, but not anything else. Hell, she would have done it regardless of whether or not it paid off her debt.

Something like sadness crossed Opal's face and she let go of Peony's arm. "It's why you don't belong here, not really. You're too good for us."

"No—"

Opal shook her head. "Not like that. As in, too nice. But we know you'll do anything to help us—that's what won us over. The fact you still helped Metcalf after he tried to kill you, it shows you're a better demon than most of us, and we respect that. Although," now Opal's gaze turned wicked, "don't repeat that. Because I don't need to get in trouble for it."

"Trouble?"

"We're assassins, we don't like *anyone*. Especially not do-gooder demons." The Radiato laughed, the sound scraping in Peony's eardrums.

She gave a strained smile in reply.

"So, when can I go back to work?" Opal asked.

"Not until I say so."

Another chuckle, and then Opal let herself out the clinic. The door had almost shut when Sylvester entered. "Nurse Sylvester, reporting for duty." He even saluted her.

Peony smiled and turned to finish typing up Opal's notes. "You're on time for once."

She hit save, then shut the laptop.

Sylvester put a hand over his heart, and a stricken expression on his face. "Me? I'm never late."

She rolled her eyes. If there was one thing she could set her clock by, it was that Sylvester would always be fifteen minutes late. That was his 'on time'. "You just have a different definition of 'late'."

"Such doubt," he said sadly.

Peony stood and headed to the door. Before she got there, he asked, "Did you talk to Dru?"

She was surprised he'd waited this long to question her. Aware there were listening spells—no such thing as patient confidentiality in her clinic—she said, "Yeah, she said she'd look into it."

The cambion nodded, but didn't look pleased. "Did she say when? She's not been around."

"She's on a mission. Trick says she'll be back any day now."

Peony had no idea what Dru was working on, and she would prefer to stay ignorant. The less she knew about the killing and pillaging, the better.

"I need to go check on my other patient," she said as Sylvester walked by her to the Mac.

He nodded as he typed in his login details.

I need to see how the pin feathers are progressing, she thought as she left the clinic.

She'd been so pleased yesterday when she'd realized that Z's wings had started to grow back. The pin feathers were tiny, and might still fall out, but it was progress, more than she'd seen in the weeks she'd been tending him.

And the look of surprise on his face...his huge emerald eyes had turned almost black with emotion, his full lips spreading open in wonder. He'd been arresting in his relief.

She'd almost bragged to her mother about his progress when Selene had called last night, but she'd caught herself in time. Aside from the fact that Peony would be courting death by spilling the beans, her mom wouldn't have been happy with the news anyway. Angels killed demons—as Z liked to point out on a regular basis—and Peony was a freak, even when it came to that.

Cambions would surely be even more of a target.

The feathers were still there!

Excitement bubbled through her as she wandered down the corridor toward the mess. Sure, Z had been acting a little strange, more aloof than normal, but she hadn't let that bother her. Maybe whatever magic-mojo Sylvester had done had helped—along with her treatments. Even the scar on Z's belly had faded a little.

She cut through the stone-walled hall, taking the shorter route. Large wooden tables dominated the expanse, with sofas and chairs set in a semi-circle near one of the massive hearths, which blazed with a fire. But the seats were largely empty—instead, a group of people hovered at the upper end of the hall, where Trick had his gaudy throne.

Not my business.

Her stomach gave a loud groan. She was starving, and she'd heard that Monica was on cooking duty, which meant there would be some kind of dessert on offer. The Foraci demon didn't cook often, but when she did...

"Quick!" Sylvester grabbed Peony's arm and dragged her into the shadows.

"What are you—?"

He held up a hand, careful not to touch her skin. "Ssshh."

She blinked.

Sylvester *never* touched her, let alone ssshhed her.

He nudged her shoulder with his own. "Look."

Trick sat on his throne, one leg thrown over the armrest, his arms crossed over his chest. The figures clustered in front of him were tall, humanoid and cloaked, and with their raised hoods, Peony couldn't see much more of them. They were ringed by a group of guild assassins, with more demons entering the hall, warily watching the newcomers. Peony could see many of their hands hovering near weapons.

What is going on?

It was rare for the Halcyon Guild to have guests—rarer still to see the banked look of aggression on Trick's face.

"We would like to purchase one of your assassins from you." The cold, cold voice swept through the hall, sending shivers down Peony's spine.

Evil.

The voice was pure evil.

Her hands trembled.

This has nothing to do with me, she told herself.

Trick uncrossed his arms. "Show me your face."

A tense silence descended on the hall, and then the speaker lowered his hood, revealing a handsome profile, with pale green skin the color of unripe olives. His long black hair was tied in a man-bun.

Dread settled into the pit of her stomach.

Her mother had shown her photos of a pure-blooded Mortus demon—and this man could be their poster child.

He wants to buy an assassin...

Dru.

The man was after Dru.

He had to be.

Mortus demons were largely insular, and they didn't buy blood slaves. They didn't need to. With their touch deadly to everyone but themselves or their mates, they had no need to hire killers. They could do the job well enough themselves.

A barely audible whistle sounded next to her ear. "Is that what I think it is?" Sylvester asked.

Peony swallowed, her throat dry. "Yes."

"Never thought I'd see a Mortus demon in my life," the cambion muttered.

She flashed him a glance.

"Well, a full-blooded one," he amended.

"You want to buy an assassin." Trick lowered his leg to the floor. "Which one? I have many."

Whispers flowed through the crowd of gathered mercenaries.

The one thing we can count on, Peony thought, *is that it's unlikely Trick will sell one of his killers.* While money was his main motivator, he also understood that loyalty was important in a place like the Halcyon Guild. If the assassins thought he'd sell them at the drop of a hat, then they wouldn't hesitate in arranging his death.

Sure, they had their blood slave bond, but he owed them his prosperity.

"She has golden skin and white hair," the Mortus said. "And she's a cambion."

"That isn't a very concise description," Trick replied.

But it was enough.

Everyone in the guild knew who the demon was referring to.

The Mortus had somehow found out about Dru, and they wanted her.

Sylvester gripped Peony's upper arm. "This is bad."

No shit, she wanted to say, but she couldn't force the words past her lips.

Trick gave the room a chilly smile. "Unfortunately, I don't have an *assassin* here that fits the profile."

No.

He wouldn't, Peony thought. *I still have decades left on my contract, and I provide an important service to the guild...*

"But I do have a healer."

CHAPTER 13

Trick had a decision to make, and fast.

Five Mortus demons stood in his hall, and he had no doubt that there were more waiting outside the guild's boundary line. *They are meant to be recluses.* It's what he had relied on for the last several decades to ensure Dru stayed off their radar. Female Mortus were rare, so he'd heard, and he hadn't wanted to lose one of his best assassins to their disgusting breeding programs.

The fact that they were here? Mortus demons did nothing without a purpose and, as direct descendants of the Hell-lord, they had the ear of Satan himself. Sure, the Halcyon Guild was in Tartarus—which meant Satan technically couldn't do anything directly to the guild, or Trick—but that didn't mean he couldn't drop by Hades' fortress and ask for a favor: like Hades coming by and telling Trick he had to deliver.

It had happened before.

Assholes.

From the Mortus' description, they clearly wanted Dru, but he couldn't let her go. She'd be used as a broodmare for those fuckers, and if that didn't work out, they'd kill her. Or try to, anyway. He didn't want her death on his conscience—not that he had much of one anymore, but still.

He didn't have many friends and he counted Dru among them.

He had to give the Mortus something; he was not going to go to war with them, and he couldn't risk them running off to Satan to get his help. Not when he had a damned angel in his cells.

Think quickly, you're running out of time.

They obviously knew he had a Mortus-cambion in his ranks. What they didn't know, clearly, was that he had two, or they'd be asking for the second as well.

His eyes skimmed over the crowd of gathered assassins, and he spotted Peony, hidden away in the shadows with Sylvester.

To the untrained eye, she was identical to Dru.

Dru will kill you for this.

Well, she'd try. Since Trick was technically her slave master, she wouldn't succeed—the blood bond would magically protect him.

I can explain it to her. She'll understand.

Hopefully.

"Unfortunately, I don't have an *assassin* here that fits the profile." Trick met the cool gaze of the lead demon and gave him a flippant smile, lying through his shiny white teeth.

He ignored the whispers that sprang to life in the crowd.

They all knew Man-bun was after Dru—and they all thought Trick was obsessed with her. Sure, he wanted to fuck her, but who didn't, if they were really honest with themselves?

Icy gray eyes surveyed Trick with an air of authority. This Mortus demon was used to getting what he wanted.

Man-bun has the same color eyes as Dru and Peony.

Maybe he's a relative.

Trick sure as Hell hoped not. The guy screamed evil—and Trick knew better than most what that meant in a demon.

Sorry, Dru.

He took a shallow breath, then said clearly, "But I do have a healer."

"A healer?" Man-bun's eyebrows rose in amusement.

Shock flared to life on Peony's face. Her features were so similar to Dru's, it was like a sucker-punch to his gut. But they were not the same woman, and Trick didn't owe Peony anything. She was valuable to the guild, he could see that, but if he had to pick his friend's life over hers...there was no choice to be made.

Plus, Peony had poisonous skin. She'd be at less risk in the Mortus den than Dru.

"She's right there." He nodded his head in Peony's direction.

He ignored the talk that erupted among his assassins. Surely they understood that it wasn't wise to piss off the Mortus? Annoying them meant annoying Satan.

Man-bun turned and looked at Peony, his expression blank except for a slight smirk. "How wonderful." He returned his attention to Trick. "How much?"

Too much, was Trick's instant reaction, but he had no choice. The guild had to survive above all else.

"That's a really good question," Trick replied.

He briefly met Peony's bruised gaze. She'd accept her fate, and make a life for herself with the Mortus, he had no doubt.

If Dru had been there, she would have been spitting fire right now, would have been ready to kill Man-bun and lay waste to the rest of his crew.

Lucky she's off hunting down a deposed god. Although, said god—Set—might not be feeling the same way, right this minute.

Peony's shoulders straightened, and she stepped away from Sylvester, who'd tried to shield her with his body.

Interesting.

"I think I'm worth at least five million bucks, wouldn't you say?" she called out.

Trick fought back a laugh.

He'd done the right thing.

CHAPTER 14

"Pack what you can, and quickly." Trick stood in her doorway, arms folded.

Peony wanted to scream at him to leave her alone, to give her this small amount of privacy, but there was no point. He wasn't going to let her out of his sight, and she knew it.

Not when five million dollars was on the line.

She'd been joking—panicked—when she'd said that amount, not really intending for the Mortus to agree to it straight away. But they had, no negotiation required.

She surveyed her room, wondering what she should take with her. There wasn't much—the bed, desk, chair and all her furniture were guild-issue and she didn't have many clothes, aside from her glove collection. Mostly she wore hospital scrubs.

Too bad I can't take my clinic with me.

And she wouldn't be able to say goodbye to Z, not with Trick hovering over her like a bad smell. Funny how that hurt more than the loss of her hard-won medical supplies.

Pulling her suitcase from her closet, she quickly assembled a mental list of what she needed to pack. Then she set about shoving her clothes, shoes and gloves into the case. At the end, she grabbed her laptop.

"That's guild property," Trick said.

She spun around, clutching the computer to her chest. "No, this is *mine.*"

He stared at her, his will powerful, trying to force her to back down. But this was a gift from her mother, and she wasn't about to leave it behind so Trick could poke around in her life. Or what was left of it.

"The clinic's computer never leaves the clinic. This is my personal property."

Trick's lips thinned, but he gave her a curt nod.

She packed the laptop away. *Do they even have the Internet where the Mortus live?* Peony paused, her hands over the case. "I just need to send a quick email—"

"No." Trick stepped further into her room. "There's no time, they're waiting for you."

Her posture straightened. "They can wait five minutes."

"I don't want the Mortus in my guild for a second longer than they need to be."

Jerk.

But she kept that thought to herself. Trick was just trying to protect the guild, and he was sacrificing her to do it. Sacrificing her to save Dru, as well, which she could understand even if she didn't like it. Dru was a more valuable asset, and a lot more hot-tempered than Peony. She'd walk into the Mortus den and start killing first, asking questions second. She'd probably be dead or in chains by the end of the first day, whereas Peony would try and make do as best she could. She didn't have Dru's fighting instincts, but she was good at making friends.

Can you really make friends with a Mortus?

That she couldn't answer. She'd become buddies—of a sort—with a Reynard's Imp, and they didn't like anyone, not even each other. The Mortus, however, were on a whole different level when it came to evildoing.

She scanned the room to see if there was anything she'd missed. There—her stethoscope. That had been a gift from her mom as well, when she'd graduated medical school. There was nothing else left. Peony didn't collect knickknacks, and she hadn't brought any of her books from home with her when she'd moved, worried they'd get stolen.

Her life really could fit into a single suitcase.

Dru is going to be so mad when she returns...

Well, that was going to be her former slave master's problem.

Mom is going to freak out if I don't email her tonight.

They kept in almost daily contact. If Peony missed a check-in, Selene would worry, and bad things happened when her mom worried. But her mother couldn't spend much time in Hell, since she was trying to keep her own existence a secret from the Hell-lords. So the guild would remain standing.

Hopefully.

Let's just pray they have Internet in the Mortus' den.

They had it in Tartarus, so why not Inferno?

She secured the lid on her leather suitcase, then let out a deep breath. Peony was about to meet her own kind for the first time. She was going to live with them, learn about them, and maybe even find a mate, although she doubted that possibility, even hoped that it wouldn't be the case.

Mortus were evil, and she...well, she wasn't.

Turning to Trick, she gripped the suitcase handle more tightly. "I'm ready."

It seemed like the whole guild was lining the hallway outside her bedroom door. Opal was closest to her, with Metcalf and Sylvester at the far end of the stone-walled corridor. Even Monica was there, her kitchen apron speckled with dark blood, her slit-pupil eyes focused on them. It looked like she had been cooking 'mystery meat' again.

Maybe it's a good thing I missed going to the mess.

As Peony walked past the assassins, the various demons nodded to her solemnly, as if they were witnessing a funeral. A lump formed in her throat, and she fought back a prickling sensation in her eyes.

She hadn't realized they all liked her this much.

Sure, Opal had implied it, and most of the demons enjoyed stopping her for a chat, but this was different. It felt like an honor guard. Even Errant was there—and it was hard to pry him away from his bookkeeping, unless he was looking for a treatment for his 'rash'.

Trick was silent beside her, an ominous shadow that kept the assassins from saying too much to her. When she reached the end of the hallway, she focused on taking deep breaths.

I will not cry.

Metcalf's shiny black eyes took in her suitcase and her

white-knuckled grip. He gave her a smile that almost made her step backward. Reynard's Imps and smiles were things that really shouldn't go together.

"You need anyone killed for you, just call me," the demon said with a nod.

She choked back a laugh. "Thanks."

Sylvester stepped forward and wrapped her in a quick but firm hug. Surprise at the physical contact rooted her to the spot; she was careful to keep the exposed skin of her face well away from the other demon. "Keep safe," he said quietly. "Don't let those fuckers take you down."

Before he pulled away, she whispered, "You take care of Z. Don't kill him, please."

That earned her a frown, but he didn't argue. Instead, those baby-blue eyes turned to Trick, darkening with rage.

Trick didn't seem to the notice the undercurrent of anger in the hall. "The Mortus are waiting."

Peony looked over her shoulder. "Thank you. All of you."

Grave nods.

Then she was walking back toward the main hall.

"Say nothing of the angel to the Mortus," Trick said, his voice low.

She flicked him a sideways glance. "You said you'd kill me if I told anyone."

"And I meant it. So, don't say anything, and you get to live."

She stopped. "You seriously think you'll be able to infiltrate the Mortus den and kill me?" Peony gave a soft, almost hysterical laugh.

"Not me personally." Trick's face was cold.

"I somewhat doubt you'll find anyone eager to do it for you."

His brown eyes flashed a warning, which she ignored.

"But don't worry. I won't blab." She shook her head. "You think the Mortus will take kindly to an unfallen angel living in Hell? *I* protect the people in my care."

She saw the barb sink home.

Satisfied, she started walking again. "Let's go; it's time for me to meet my new master."

CHAPTER 15

Careful of his injured wing, Z stretched the appendage up and over his shoulder, marveling at the tiny pin feathers that had emerged. Scabs and abscesses still marred the bones of his wings, but they were trying to regenerate.

I won't have to have them cut off.

A wave of relief shot through him. Trick's threat had weighed heavily the past few weeks, to the point where he'd almost begged the little healer to cut his wings off for him. That way Z could move on—drive the self-pity from his mind and focus on healing the rest of his body so he could escape.

He hadn't been able to make the request, because while there was a possibility they'd grow back, there was also the chance he would lose his wings forever. Z hadn't been able to fully face that future.

To be fair, he doubted she would have done it, had he managed to voice the words. She'd seemed convinced she could save his wings; and she'd been right. They still had a long way to go, but they *were* healing, and he was going to be whole again, provided no one else decided to hurt him.

I won't let them.

He wasn't sure how he would achieve that, being as weak as a kitten, but he would try.

More accurately, his mind whispered, she *won't let them hurt you.*

His little healer.

No, she'd fight for him tooth and nail, he knew it.

He swept his wing back to its resting position, pressing his cheek against the stone floor, welcoming the grittiness of the earth. He missed the skies, the clouds and eddies of Heaven, but at least here he could feel the pulse of the world underneath him. Z knew it was partly because he was sensation-deprived; he needed to feel *something.*

She said no touching.

And that made him want to touch her all the more.

Maybe that's why she did it, to try and generate interest.

There were plenty of demons who he could imagine trying to manipulate him like that, but he didn't think she was one of them. And to do that, she had to know he found her...pretty. Hopefully, he'd never indicated that to her.

You've gone crazy because of your head injury. Finding a demon attractive.

No, he thought, being honest with himself. *She's attractive, and I'm male.* Sure, she didn't have the painful perfection that Dina possessed, but he liked that about the healer. She was more real, more...attainable.

The few times he'd been with Dina, it had been a meeting of bodies, nothing more than him scratching an itch for a powerful woman. Or perhaps easing her curiosity more than anything else. He'd been in half in love with her the first time, but her coolness afterward had served as a shock—she'd liked him enough to bed him, but not keep him.

And it had been the right attitude, he could see that now.

They probably should have never been intimate anyway, them both being Darts. If the others had known, they would have not approved. Azrael in particular—he'd lived for the cause. Z had never even heard the angel's name linked with another's, just practice, practice and practice. Raziel was secretive, so Z wouldn't have known even if he had a lover, but Seraphina and Yael had been known to enjoy earthly matters. He'd even heard a rumor that Seraphina had been close to entering an understanding with another angel.

I wonder what they are all doing now.

He hoped searching for him was on the top of their list.

What if they think you're dead?

His muscles clenched in protest at the thought. Why hadn't he considered that before? Unless there was any proof he was still alive, they might very well believe him dead, might have already moved on with their lives.

The door to Z's cell clanged open and the Incubus—Sylvester—stood there wearing a thunderous frown.

Z tried to look past him, for the healer.

"She's not with me," Sylvester said, dragging in the torture cart with the familiar sound of rattling glass and clanging metal. The demon's blue eyes were cold.

"What do you mean?" Z propped himself on his

elbows, wincing as his arms shook from the strain. He doubted he could even do one pushup, now.

How the mighty have fallen.

Shush.

He had to concentrate on the demon.

Something like rage flittered across the Incubus' face. "She's gone."

Z frowned.

The little healer wouldn't have just walked away from him—uh, her job. She was too dedicated.

"What do you mean, 'She's gone'?"

Sylvester snapped on a pair of plastic gloves. "My statement was pretty clear. I don't think it needs clarification."

Without the healer to smooth things over, Z realized Sylvester did not feel kindly toward him. From the tension in the demon's muscles and his pursed-mouthed look of distaste, it was clear the Incubus would prefer to be anywhere but here.

"She just left?" Z asked, disbelieving.

Sylvester sighed. "Not exactly."

He waited. Patience was supposedly a virtue, and he didn't want the demon knowing he was dying to know the answer.

Bad choice of words.

Sylvester bent over Z's wings, methodically inspecting them and dabbing on an astringent-smelling liquid from time to time. The medicine stung, but the silence—it burned.

The Incubus was packing up his equipment when he said, "She was sold."

Truth.

Z's head whipped toward the demon. "What do you mean?"

"Some demons came looking for someone who fit her description. She was sold to them as a result."

He growled. "She's a person, you can't sell—"

Wait, was he *defending* a demon?

How the other Darts would have laughed at him...then taken him away for a mental-health check. He—like all angels—had been very much of the opinion that demons were evil, angels were good, and that *all* demons should die.

Now he'd done a complete turnaround.

But the healer is different.

She was compassionate and genuine, and nothing like what he'd been told demons were like. She deserved more than to be sold like chattel.

Sylvester let out a bitter laugh. "Almost everyone here is a blood slave, yourself included. Slaves are nothing more than commodities to be used or sold. Get used to it. It's your life now." His pure blue eyes went cold. "If you survive, that is."

Truth. All of it.

Including the part where Z was also a blood slave. Trick had said the same, but everything about Trick was a strange mixture of lies and truth, so Z hadn't really believed him.

I don't remember signing any documents.

But he'd been barely conscious when he'd arrived, and Trick was a slimy bastard at the best of times. He could have forged Z's signature easily.

Can demons even hold angels as slaves?

He had no idea.

Raziel would probably be able to answer the question—he'd been a scholar before the silver filaments in his wings had indicated he was warrior caste. But Raziel was as far away as Heaven was from Hell, and he had no way of contacting the other angel now his telepathic connection didn't seem to work.

After Sylvester left, Z lay with his head on his forearms.

The healer has been sold.

What would happen to her? What kind of demons had purchased her? And how had she ended up in this guild in the first place?

Maybe he should have been wondering that since day one.

You shouldn't care.

No, he shouldn't.

It didn't change the fact that he did, *and* that he owed her his wings. He had no doubt that, if not for her care, he might have been wingless or dead. Or both.

You owe her a debt.

And so what that he wanted to repay her with more than just his gratitude? That he had a consuming need to know what her skin felt like, to understand what really drove her to help people.

You're a fool.

He wasn't going to argue with himself over that.

Z's eyelids grew heavy, and as he drifted off to sleep, trying work out how to free himself and then help the healer, Sylvester's words ran through his mind.

Why had the demon's final statement seemed more like a threat than an explanation?

CHAPTER 16

The Mortus were waiting for her near the guild's stone-lined entry, a group of tan-cloaked individuals who stood eerily quiet and motionless. Only the leader with the man-bun had his hood down.

Peony fought the fear that threatened to swamp her. *Change is as good as a holiday, they say.*

'They' are idiots.

There was no false cheer for her.

She could remember the first day she'd stepped through the metal doors to the guild—clutching a suitcase in one hand, much as she was doing now, her contract tightly held in the other. She'd been in shock at discovering she had a twin, and the fact that Dru had almost killed her mother.

It was only through signing her life away as a slave to Trick that Peony had been able to save her mom. *I should probably hate Dru for that.* But she couldn't. Dru had come after a woman who she'd thought had killed their birth mother, only to discover that Peony was alive and loved. Raised with care. And that Selene had tried to salvage a situation gone bad.

Peony had been too late to stop Dru poisoning Selene with bloomshade, a rare poison from Sheol, but she'd given her the key to the antidote: Trick. He had had the cure in his 'special collection' and had refused to give it away for anything other than Peony's soul.

It was the least she could do for the mother who had saved her life.

And, well, part of her thought it might result in her and Dru growing closer. That hadn't quite gone according to plan. Oh, they weren't strangers anymore, but they still weren't...friends. Peony wasn't sure that Dru even *had* any friends.

But on that long-ago day, when Peony had stood in the entryway, fresh out of the Human Realm, she hadn't known what to expect, or how to act in an assassins guild. She'd never even been to Hell before.

Here I go, starting over again.

Except this time, it would be worse.

Much worse.

She'd avoided attracting the Mortus' attention for a reason. Sure, most of the information about the demon race had come from her mother, but Selene didn't lie. Not often, anyway. Dru had been just as adamant that they stay away from their father's race, and well, there wasn't much out there that frightened her sister.

'The Mortus are direct descendants of Satan. They only do what is in their best interest, and they keep their women like slaves.' Dru's voice rang through her head as the Mortus demons turned to face her.

"We are ready." The cold voice belonged to the Mortus demon with the man-bun, his gaze sweeping over

Peony's body from head to toe. His eyes lingered on her gloved hands for a few seconds; a flicker of confusion passed over his face then disappeared.

She took a deep breath, then exhaled it quietly. She fought the shiver that proximity to the Mortus gave her—she could *feel* their evil, just like she could sense Z's inherent goodness.

Do it. Take a step forward. Now or never.

Peony would have preferred never, but she wasn't a coward. She had to do this, for Dru, for the guild. There was a reason the Mortus demons were some of the most feared in the underworld—they would try to destroy everyone at the Halcyon Guild if she refused to leave now.

Trick wouldn't let her out of the deal he'd made, anyway.

Five million dollars was nothing to sneeze at.

"It's time," Trick said quietly next to her.

She refused to look at him. Just because she understood what he'd done, it didn't mean she liked it—or him.

Peony lifted her chin. "Fine."

One of the Mortus approached to take her suitcase. She pulled her hand away. "I can carry it."

Man-bun shook his head. "Hand it over."

Wanting to argue, but knowing it was likely futile, she reluctantly passed over all her worldly possessions.

Quicker than she could follow, she was spun around and her arms grabbed and wrenched behind her back. Her wrists were tied together before she could even manage a startled "What?"

"We don't want to take any unnecessary chances," the

lead demon said when she turned back to face him. One of the cloaked figures moved away from her.

Her arms hurt in their new position, the ache twinging in her shoulders and wrists.

Man-bun reached into his cloak and then flung out a hand of glittery dust. Before it settled to the ground, he drew a small circle in the air and muttered a few words in a language she didn't understand. A Devilsgate sprung to life in the middle of the foyer, the circular portal bordered by a glimmering red light.

Wow.

This Mortus demon had serious money, to be able to call up a Devilsgate like that, or he had serious magic himself. Either option was worrying. Peony didn't have any magic at all and she had a total of fifty dollars to her name. How would she manage to get away—if she ever needed to—when they could do *that*?

"Vin," the Mortus directed, "you go through first."

One of the cloaked demons nodded and stepped through the gate. The lead demon then waved at the others. Peony watched as her suitcase disappeared through the magical portal, a small lump forming in the back of her throat. This was it. She was leaving her home of the last ten years.

Leaving Sylvester and Metcalf...and Dru.

Leaving Z.

Shutting her eyes, she told herself that the last part didn't matter. He was an angel and he was finally healing on his own. He'd recover, and then he'd forget about her entirely. It was just her stupid fault for being too...attached to her patient.

The lead Mortus strode forward and took hold of one

of Peony's trapped arms. "It's our turn now."

Something feral slid across his face when she turned to meet his gaze, and she barely repressed a shudder. Where his hand touched her arm, she could *feel* the evil in him. His grip tightened briefly, and then he guided her toward the portal.

She didn't look back as they stepped through. Not when it was only Trick to see her off.

Her skin tingled as the magical portal deposited them somewhere dark. It took a few moments for her eyesight to adjust to the dim lighting.

I'm in a cave.

The walkway beneath their feet was slightly undulating, and the walls were carved into what appeared to be basalt.

She'd entered the Mortus' den.

Mom is going to kill me.

Well, Selene would probably kill Trick first.

I don't think I'd be too unhappy about that.

And for once, the idea of someone dying didn't bother her. Not after Trick had thrown her under a bus. It'd be what he deserved.

How many other members of the guild had he screwed over?

Not your business anymore.

No.

"Come along." The Mortus pulled her down the hall to a T-intersection. Strange writing was carved into the wall before her, and if she squinted just right, it was almost like she could read it. Which was strange. She'd never seen its kind before.

The hand tightened on her bicep, but the lead demon's

voice didn't sound annoyed. "Stop delaying."

She shot him a look, surprised to see his face wore a blank expression, almost like he was bored by the whole buying-a-cambion-and-taking-her-back-to-his   lair business.

"What kind of writing is that?" she asked.

He tilted his head slightly. "It's an ancient angelic dialect."

"Why do you have angelic script *here*?" She asked, then bit her lip. That sounded almost rude, but it was a valid question.

She stared at the carved writing. The symbols reminded her a little of ancient Greek and Latin, but they were unique all the same. A few words filtered through her mind: 'scion of Heaven', 'depths of Hell'.

She blinked and they vanished.

How had —?

A gentle push against her arm, the movement surprising her. "Come, you may stare at this script later on if you so desire."

Something had changed in the demon's face, and she didn't know what had caused it.

He led Peony down a series of tunnels, some with the angelic letters carved into the walls, some without. They soon arrived in a small white-painted chamber with an art-deco hearth and a series of Edwardian drawing-room chairs lined up around its perimeter. It was...cozy.

They stopped near the hearth. Behind her, one of the guards set her suitcase down near the entry, while another demon came in through a side door. He was dressed in a Victorian-era suit, complete with lace adornments, cravat, waistcoat and jacket. He wore a silver circlet like a crown and his long black hair was threaded with gray. She could clearly see the similarity between his features and the Mortus standing next to her.

He wore no gloves, but she didn't doubt he was deadly.

The royal Mortus stopped abruptly when he spotted her, jabbing out a finger.

"*You*!" His face turned a mottled purple.

"Me?" She hadn't meant for her voice to sound so timid.

Quicker than she could track, he was before her. Rage made his gray eyes glitter, and his hand was swinging toward her face in a backhanded slap. Faster than she believed possible, she pulled back before his bare skin touched her cheek, her neck protesting the sudden movement.

"I wouldn't do that, if I were you," she said. *Not unless you want to die,* she added in her head. It sounded over dramatic, even then.

"Bitch, you will take whatever punishment I deem worthy." Spittle flew from his mouth, and the atmosphere of the room pulsed with his rage.

Peony frowned, not understanding. "Punishment for what?"

What did Dru *do*?

CHAPTER 17

You need to make a plan, Z thought.

Now he was finally healing, he would be let out of his cell. Once free, he'd try to make a break for it. Not that he knew which part of Hell he was being held in, but he'd work it out. He'd been in worse situations before—he just couldn't remember one right now. Training to qualify as a member of the Darts had been tough; being dropped naked in a human forest filled with guerrilla fighters and with his wings bound hadn't been a walk in the park.

At least you have clothes now.

If you could call the light-blue trousers clothes. He had no shirt, since his wings were in the way, no socks and no underwear.

Try and do a push up.

Yes, he'd need to get some physical conditioning back to make his escape.

Planting his hands on the stone floor and balancing his weight on his tiptoes, he gave a heave up, and grinned. Yes!

A moment later, his arms wobbled and he dropped

back to the floor with a dull thud.

He lay there panting, frustration zinging through his blood.

The door opened slowly.

Z glowered at the stone floor against his face. It wasn't time for Trick's regular gloat, and Sylvester had just left. He lifted his head and froze in surprise.

The healer. She was back!

The shock of white hair and golden skin made his heart gallop in his chest, and his eyes roved hungrily over her from head to toe.

But something wasn't...*right*.

Gone were her customary blue shirt and trousers; instead she wore black pants and a tank top that hugged her figure. Her hands were glove-free, something he had never seen before, and her gray eyes were cold, calculating, her mouth pressed in a flat line.

She looked hard. Nothing like the demon he was used to dealing with.

Realization hit him. "You aren't...*her*."

She couldn't be, even though they looked near identical. No one changed that much in a day or two.

Unless she was always like that and had been pretending.

Normally he would have considered that an option, but not his healer. She was utterly genuine.

"No, I'm her sister."

His head dropped back to the floor. "She's gone."

"Want to help me get her back?" The healer's sister leaned against the door frame like she had all the time in the world.

A bitter chuckle rose inside. Him? Help? He couldn't even do one push up! No matter that he'd been planning his escape and her rescue not long ago.

"What am I going to be able to do?" Z asked.

"Well, you are an angel. And you aren't fallen."

"I may as well be."

"You have wings."

He snorted and moved the partially ruined flesh.

"They look like they're growing back. And I might know a guy who can help you."

He fought the feeling of hope that slammed into him. Her sister was a healer...it was true they may know someone.... "What are you saying?"

"Come with me," the woman said.

"And go where?" If he was a blood-bound slave, it wasn't like he could just head out the front door.

"To a friend's."

"I'm not really in any condition to walk." Or even crawl, if truth were told.

She waved a hand, dismissing his concern, and stepped further into the room. "First, we make a deal."

A deal. Of course. Nothing was free with a demon.

"Like what?" he asked. She may be his healer's sister, but they were *nothing* alike, he could sense that now.

"That you have to help me find Peony when you're well."

Peony.

It suited her. Soft, beautiful and honorable, as with the Chinese translation.

Funny how he'd never known her name, and yet he could picture the exact shade of her eyes, the color of her skin...

He nodded. "Deal."

A tingle spread out along his spine as the magic of the

promise took hold.

The demon gave him a brief, fierce grin. "Let's go."

He thought he was going to vomit.

Breathe in, breathe out. That's it.

Swallow.

Z dropped to his knees on a blanket of bright-green grass, breathing air that smelled of flowers and hydrocarbons.

They were no longer in Hell.

Maybe I should lie down. His body collapsed onto his stomach before he'd finished the thought.

"That was not fun," he muttered against the astringent grass.

A low chuckle sounded, and then Peony's sister gave him an awkward pat on the shoulder. "If you're going to puke, try not to do it on my shoes."

He turned his face to the side and glared at her. "A little warning would have been useful."

His body had not been up to the rigors of teleportation. And that hadn't felt like any teleportation he'd ever experienced before. It certainly hadn't been a Devilsgate, either.

Can Peony do that, too?

She gave a negligent shrug, but her eyes were wary. "It wasn't like I was going to walk you out the front door," she said, her statement echoing his earlier thought. "Trick would have had us killed on the spot."

Z sighed. "You, maybe. Me, he wants."

A twisted smile graced her face. "Oh, little do you

know." She chuckled, but it sounded off. "Now, you need to lie here like a good little angel and wait for me to come and get you."

He rose up on his elbows. All he could see was garden—grass edged with gravel-lined paths and a hedge. "What if we're in danger?"

She raised a shoulder and held out her hands, palm up. "You could poke them?"

He blew out a steady stream of air and counted to five silently. Surely she could see that leaving him flat out in someone's garden was not the best idea? Especially if they were in the Human Realm.

Angels were meant to be secret, after all. Except in a religious context.

"That is not an adequate plan," he finally replied.

"Don't stress. Even if something happens to me, they'll come get you."

Truth, at least as far as she believed it.

Who was this 'friend'?

Anyway, he wasn't stressed, he was concerned for their safety. They were two totally different things.

Z frowned. "I don't understand."

"You don't have to."

"What's your name?" he blurted.

She pursed her lips. "Oh yeah. That might help. I'm Dru."

"Call me Z," he replied.

She nodded. "Just hang tight."

Hang-what?

But she was gone, her step confident as she disappeared around a hedge.

How can she and Peony be so different?

A few minutes later he heard her shout, "Touch me and I'll cut you a new fucking smile!"

He struggled to rise to his hands and knees. He would help, she was clearly in trouble.

Then heard a growled, "Motherfucker!"

That voice sounded eerily familiar, but the profanity was so out of context he struggled to reconcile the new information.

A new speaker entered the fray, this one also blessedly familiar. "*Yael*!"

"Shit!"

The sounds of scuffling and grunting came over the hedge, but he was too weak to even make it to his knees, never mind peer over the top.

Useless, you're useless.

He hung his head in shame. Low murmurs of a conversation were taking place some distance away. He couldn't make out the words, but the anger seemed to have fled the situation. He hoped Dru was okay, or he was going to spend a cold night in the garden. Plus Peony would be upset to learn he'd done nothing while her twin was injured.

His arms shook from holding himself up and he dropped to his side, spreading a wing out on the springy grass.

So weak.

A few minutes later, Dru appeared, her shirt torn and dirt smeared across one cheek.

"What happened?"

"Eh, my friend's housemate is an asshole."

That didn't answer the question. At least, not clearly.

Dru grabbed one of his arms and slung it over her

shoulder. The contact was shocking to him, like being near Peony, but not. His heartbeat stayed regular and he wasn't curious about her softness, even though she looked identical to his healer.

"Ready? I'm gonna haul you up. I'll need your help—you're heavy for someone who is skinny enough to make Opal horny."

He had no idea who Opal was, but he didn't want to make her horny.

Taking a deep breath, he put every ounce of his energy in getting upright. "Is one of their name's Yael?"

She grunted and then they were standing. Well, he was half-drooping. Dru was stronger than she looked.

Just like Peony.

Dru flicked him a glance. "Yeah, the asshole."

Looking over the top of the hedge, Z stared at the two men watching them. One had long dark hair tied back loosely from a chiseled face; the other had brown hair cut military-short.

The Darts. Azrael and Yael.

Tears burned his eyes, and he struggled to breathe.

He'd found them.

Azrael sprinted toward to them, clutching at his side, as if he were injured. Then he was beside them.

Where are his wings?

Idiot. They must be concealed by magic. We're in the Human Realm, after all.

"*Zadkiel?*" Azrael's expression held traces of horror as his gaze swept over Z's sunken and tortured body.

He nodded, afraid he'd cry if he spoke.

He was a warrior angel, not a child with a skinned knee.

Azrael draped Z's free arm over his shoulder, and they hobbled toward an enormous white mansion, up its front stairs and into a foyer. Every part of his body hurt, but he was free, and he was with his fellow Darts. Yael was close behind them, holding out what looked like a cellphone. He also sent out a deafening mental blast.

'Zadkiel is here!'

Wonder consumed him, temporarily drowning out the pain. *I can hear them.*

His brain hadn't been permanently damaged from the head wound.

So, something in the guild prevented me from calling out.

It was a thought he would have to ponder later.

Dru and Azrael carefully laid Zadkiel on a backless sofa, and he couldn't conceal the grunt of discomfort that accompanied the movement. He briefly met Azrael's gaze and looked away, not liking the pity he saw in those blue eyes.

"Where did you find him?" Azrael asked Dru.

"My guild had him."

"What? You knew the whole time—?"

The whole time? Z watched them both; their body language was too familiar for casual acquaintances. What had happened between these two?

"I had heard we had an angel captured, but I didn't know he was your friend. I still had no idea when I removed him from the guild."

Truth.

Z had never said anything, and he'd only told her his name after they left...

Azrael shut his eyes. "But you brought him here anyway."

"It was the only safe place I could think of for an angel."

Truth.

When had the Darts become friends with demons?

He'd thought they would ostracize him for his...compassion for Peony. But it seemed like his comrades had been doing something similar.

They probably befriended demons in order to find you.

Guilt sat heavy in his stomach.

It would have enraged Azrael to have to play nice with a demon.

"You stole the Orb," Yael accused Dru.

Peony's sister turned to the other angel, her eyes bleeding black, evil seeping from her. Z bit his lip—he'd never seen, or felt, that happen with Peony.

"It was part of my mission," Dru said. "And it was going to buy my sister's and my freedom."

So they are both slaves?

"Freedom?" Yael asked.

"I was a blood slave. So is my sister."

"What happened to your sister?" Azrael asked, moving closer to Dru.

Z tried to appear like he wasn't as interested in the answer as he was. However, his whole body strained to hear her response.

Dru's eyes held an inky darkness that was all-consuming. "Trick sold her to the Mortus."

The Mortus?

"He betrayed me," Dru added.

Truth.

"You betrayed us," Yael snapped.

Peony would never have done that, Z thought.

Dru nodded, the black receding from her eyes. "I did. But only for our freedom. I would have tried to help after. And, well, here." Dru reached into her pack and pulled out a cloth-wrapped bundle. She shoved it at Azrael.

The other Dart grabbed it automatically, and then his eyes widened as he unwrapped it, exposing a red-golden ball that glowed with an inner fire.

"Is that—?" Yael whispered.

"It's the Orb."

The what?

CHAPTER 18

"You need to be punished for killing my men!" the royal Mortus shouted.

"I haven't killed anyone," she said slowly.

The demon's face turned a darker shade of aubergine as his hands formed fists at his side. "You think you can lie to me, *whore*? I saw you do it!"

"I have never seen you before in my life," Peony protested. Not unless she had done something in her sleep, and somnambulance was not a trait she could admit to. "It wasn't me."

"One scratch of those claws and—"

Peony started shaking her head. "I don't have any claws!"

Her interruption made the demon lose control. He punched her in the stomach, then clipped her over the shoulders with another jab. The pain was instant, firing her nerves. She vomited bile right on his feet, bitterness lingering in her mouth, as she stayed bent over, fighting for breath.

A body partially moved between them. "Stop!"

"Godric, you *dare* interfere?"

A grunt, and the royal figure stepped back. A pair of legs moved into her line of vision, cloak flowing around them.

"One moment, Uncle, I just want to check something."

"If you stop me from beating obedience into this whore one more time..."

A gloved finger tilted her chin up. "You didn't want my uncle touching your skin before. Why?"

She swallowed back more stomach acid and grimaced as her whole abdomen throbbed. "My skin, it's toxic."

Someone scoffed. "You passed the skin test."

"And I said I've never seen you before! It wasn't me!" The protest was out before she could call it back. She prepared for another blow, but the younger demon stayed between her and the royal, like a bodyguard.

"You say you've never seen us before. Your skin is toxic." The younger demon picked up one of her gloved hands—the movement almost...gentle. "You said you don't have claws?"

She *could* pretend to be her sister, so they wouldn't try and track Dru down as well, but there was no point. Peony might not be toxic to other Mortus, but she had tested her venom in a laboratory situation and it was the most virulent toxin on the planet. She wasn't about to take the risk. One touch on her bare skin and someone could die—or be in agony for hours. And if Dru had killed someone here already...

Peony wasn't a murderer.

"No, I don't have claws," she said.

He dropped her hand.

"She lies," the uncle hissed.

"I have a sister," Peony said. "Her name is Dru. She has claws and is an assassin for the guild you just purchased me from."

She then met the Godric's gaze. "We are twins, but we are not one hundred percent identical. I don't have claws and my skin is toxic to touch, like a normal Mortus."

The purple mottling began to fade from the older demon's skin as he considered her words. His switch from palpable rage to calm consideration was unnerving.

"There's *two* of you?" he blurted.

Peony fought an inappropriate smile. "I take it Dru visited here recently?"

Godric stepped back. "She left a number of dead bodies in her wake."

Sounds like her.

Perhaps they were meant to balance each other—Dru the killer, Peony the healer. No. That sounded too much like fate for her liking, and she didn't want to believe in that.

It meant somewhere, someone divine didn't like her.

The royal demon's skin had returned to its normal olive-green hue. "Prove you aren't your sister."

"The only way I can do that is if I touch someone," Peony replied slowly. "And I don't want to hurt anyone."

They stared at her.

"You don't want to hurt anyone?" the royal parroted, like the concept was something he'd never considered before.

"No, I'm a healer. And there is a risk my toxin could harm someone..."

Godric ran a hand over his hair. "Dru's toxin killed several Mortus outright."

Peony blanched. "Then my touch will be just as deadly."

If Dru was more poisonous than the normal Mortus, Peony would be even more so. She didn't even need a cut to deposit her venom into a victim, skin contact was enough.

"Prove it," the royal demanded.

She shook her head.

Godric faced the other demon. "Uncle, we just lost several men. Who would we spare?"

"Some of the men have expressed their displeasure at our handling of the situation. I think a lesson may be in order." His cold resolve was plain in every word.

Peony stepped back.

"You will prove yourself, girl. Or you will die. Either option is perfectly fine with me."

She clenched her fists. "But they'll die."

He shook his head, like she was simple. "Death is inevitable; and when you're Mortus, it comes at my will. Something for you to remember."

They paid five million dollars for me, only to kill me at the first instance?

It made no sense.

The royal turned away and barked for one of the loitering cloaked men to come forward. He issued a series of orders Peony couldn't hear, then turned back to her. The room emptied, leaving just him and Godric.

"My name is King Alvin Mortimus Severus deSatan, this is my nephew, Godric."

Her eyes widened. Alvin had actually included the Hell-lord as part of his name.

The Mortus are the direct descendants of Satan.

That was the rumor, at any rate.

Apparently the king believed it was the truth. That or he had brass balls, as Dru would say.

"Who were your parents?" Godric asked.

"My mother was human and she died at my birth. I don't know the identity of my father." Not for lack of trying to find out. Selene hadn't liked Peony's need to learn the identity of her sire, but she hadn't prevented her search. Dru had also looked, but it was like their parent had vanished from the face of the earth.

Which probably wasn't a bad thing, considering his species.

Godric stepped away from her and her vomit, now that the apparent danger to her had passed. "Do you possess magic for healing?"

"No, I studied medicine in the Human Realm."

Alvin's brows furrowed together. "You did *what*?"

Were these people hard of hearing?

"I became a doctor," she clarified.

"A Mortus became a doctor." Horror masked the king's features. "Imagine if any other species found out..."

Godric shook his head. "She's a cambion, people expect them to be...odd."

"At least the other one was properly behaved."

Properly behaved? Murdering a bunch of people was acceptable, but helping them wasn't?

Mom was right. They are all psychopaths.

Not that she had really doubted it, but this conversation felt surreal.

A knock on the door made them turn. Two of the cloaked men were back, with a Mortus male standing between them.

"Your Majesty wishes to see me?" the newcomer asked.

"Lord Farcon, such a pleasure to see you. How do you fare after your brother's demise? Does the new title sit well?" An oily smile creased the king's mouth.

Peony's stomach churned uneasily, and not just because of its recent vomiting.

The new arrival's eyes settled on Peony and he lunged forward, only to be held back by the cloaked figures.

"Bitch!" he shouted.

Great, another one of Dru's acquaintances.

CHAPTER 19

"You didn't hand it over to Trick?" Azrael asked, referring to this mysterious Orb.

Dru shook her head.

Hurried footsteps sounded in the hall and then Raziel and Seraphina burst into the room, Raziel in a tailored suit, Seraphina in an expensive looking dress.

They were clothed like humans.

And, like Yael and Azrael, Z noticed, their wings were hidden from sight.

They must have gone undercover to find us.

Was Dina with them?

Seraphina and Raziel locked their eyes on Z, their shouts and cries of surprise deafening in the small room. They hurried toward him, Seraphina running gentle hands over the skin of his back, careful to avoid his ruined wings.

He tried not to flinch. He didn't want her hands on him, he realized. He wanted Peony's.

There is something wrong with you.

"Oh, Zadkiel, what did they do to you?" The pity in

Seraphina's voice was like being doused with a bucket of cold water.

Wasn't it obvious? "They plucked my wings."

But he had survived.

He was here.

He hadn't given up.

He didn't deserve pity, he deserved praise.

Raziel placed a tentative hand on one of Z's shoulders, then focused his attention on the glowing sphere in Azrael's hand. "She brought you the Orb?" the dark-skinned angel asked.

"And Zadkiel," Azrael replied.

Raziel nodded at Dru. "Thank you. But why?"

Typical Raziel. Polite to a fault. The angel's thoughts were unreadable, as always.

"My sister was sold to the Mortus," Dru said. "She was caring for your buddy, helping him heal. We made a deal. He's going to help me get her back. And I thought I should return the Orb to you. You need it more than I do."

"Thank you," Azrael said, staring at Dru like she was a miracle.

Tingles spread all over Z's skin. What was going on here? Azrael *hated* demons. And now he was...friendly with one?

Very friendly from the appearance of things.

What had happened to the Darts in his absence?

"That's lovely and all," Yael cut in. "But we can't use it."

"No one can," Seraphina said.

"*What*?" Dru snapped.

"Only a demon who is 'pure of heart' can use the Orb,"

Azrael explained.

Dru pivoted on her heel and looked at Z.

He didn't know what this Orb did, but if only the pure of heart could use it... "The little healer," he said.

Dru nodded. "My sister."

Yael laughed. "There is no such thing as a demon who is 'pure of heart'."

Now *that* sounded more like the Darts he had left in Heaven.

"Peony was raised by humans," Dru said. "She went to medical school, intending to become a doctor. She just wants to help people."

"She is kind. Pure," Z added and struggled to rise. Raziel and Seraphina pressed him back into the sofa. "We must save her."

"You must heal first," Seraphina said.

And who knew how long that would take? It had already been months since his capture.

Azrael and Dru walked out of the room, gazing at each other like they were starving.

A temporary silence descended in the wake of their departure, and he could feel the other Darts staring at his ruined wings.

Get used to it.

"Is Dina here?" Z asked.

Their attention shifted from his body to his face.

Raziel's expression was serious. "No. We haven't heard anything about Dina since you were both taken. We were hoping you knew what happened to her."

Gone, she's gone.

A pit formed in his gut. He may not have the romantic feelings he once possessed for the other angel, but she had been his commander and a fine one at that. She had been a force to be reckoned with in Heaven for centuries. To have lost her...

"We were together on guard duty, but then we were attacked." He didn't want to admit the whole story, it painted him too badly, but these angels were his comrades. They deserved the truth, to know what a failure he had been. "I was knocked unconscious early into the fight."

"Do you know who attacked?" Yael asked, his voice calm.

Z studied him. Yael had never been particularly cool-natured. What had changed him?

"Infernus demons," Z replied.

"*What*?" Seraphina's outburst was followed by curses from Raziel and Yael. She turned to the other dark-skinned angel. "Raze, Infernus are bad. For them to get into Heaven..."

Raze?

Stern, storm-colored eyes met Z's briefly. Then Raziel focused on Seraphina. "Lucifer was once an angel and one of their ancestors. It is possible he knew of a way to penetrate Heaven's defenses."

"But why wait millennia?" Yael demanded.

"That I cannot answer."

Neither could Z. As if he would have any real concept of why a Hell-lord behaved the way they did; evil had its own motivations.

"If the Infernus have Dina, they will be difficult to track," Yael said, then he disappeared into the hall outside the room. He returned wearing a disgusted expression. "Who would have thought?"

"What?" Raze asked.

"Azrael and that *demon*." Yael shook his head. "He could have had an archangel."

"A *what*?" Z blurted.

He hadn't thought Azrael had any interest in romance at all.

"Aurora came to us not long ago and offered Azrael a position as consort," Yael explained.

Raziel rolled his eyes, which knocked Z off balance. Raziel was never anything but collected. "And I told you, I think it was a set up. They wanted the Orb. She would have backed out of the deal once he handed it over."

"She's an *archangel*," Yael protested.

"And look what the others did to us," Raziel said. "You really think she would have taken one of us as a consort?"

Seraphina and Yael flinched.

What had happened to them?

"Why do you still hide your wings?" Z asked, struggling to sit. Raziel helped him upright with gentle but strong hands. Once he was no longer flat on his belly, the others stood in front of him, acceptance and anger warring in their expressions.

Seraphina's deep brown eyes met his. "When it was discovered that the Inner Sanctum had been breached, we were punished."

An icy wave washed through his veins. "The Sanctum was breached?"

They nodded.

"Heaven's Heart was stolen," Raziel said quietly.

"*No.*"

To lose both Dina and the Heart...

He had failed. Truly and utterly.

Heaven would never forgive him. He was an exile.

Maybe that's why my wings had so much trouble healing. I am no longer a true angel.

"As punishment for the Darts' failure," Raziel continued, "we were exiled from Heaven, and our wings removed."

"*What*?" Horror made his vision fade to gray.

They were *fallen*?

Because of *him*?

Please let this be a nightmare.

He blinked, rubbed his arms, even pinched the lax muscle on his thigh...but the three of them still stood before him, wearing the same expressions, their feathers no more in evidence than they were a minute prior.

He had cost his comrades their wings.

"I am so sorry," Z croaked.

Raziel placed a gentle hand on his shoulder. "It is not your fault."

"How can you say that? I was on duty. Heaven was breached, the Heart was stolen and *you* lost your wings for it."

He was clearly to blame.

"Dina was also there, and she is a squadron worth of soldiers in herself," Yael said. "I have never seen her equal in war, not even Azrael."

Azrael was renowned for his prowess with almost any weapon, but Dina was a force to be reckoned with.

"Dina and I failed," Z said.

"And you clearly have been punished for it," Seraphina said, eyeing his broken wings. Wings he'd been so proud of not an hour or so before.

Now they made him feel nothing but guilt.

"Could yours grow back?" he asked.

Raziel shook his head. "They were removed by archangels. Only they can grant them back."

"But why did they take them?" Betrayal lanced through him.

"To set an example," Yael said and snorted in disgust. "No matter that none of the other patrols were punished. Just us."

"You know they have their reasons," Seraphina argued.

"Now you see why Azrael did not take Aurora up on her offer," Raziel said to Yael. "We could not trust that she was not working against the other archangels. They are the voices of God, but they do have their own politics."

Yael just crossed his arms over his chest.

The room fell silent a moment then Raziel clapped his hands. "First thing's first. We will get Zadkiel healed, then worry about Dina and our wings later."

"It's Z."

"Sorry?" Raziel looked at him.

"I go by Z now, not Zadkiel."

A slow nod. "And I am now called Raze."

Strangely, it suited the suit-clad angel.

"You can still call me Yael," Yael said with a smirk.

Seraphina shook her head in exasperation. "Useful as always."

"Hey!" Yael raised an eyebrow. "You haven't changed your name either. Although I do like Sera. Sexy Sera."

She ignored him, addressing Z instead. "If our first action is to get Z well again, I know a healer we can use."

She gestured to his wings.

Shock kept him quiet. He seriously doubted there were any healers who could repair the damage to his wings, and he didn't want to hope.

Couldn't afford to.

CHAPTER 20

Seraphina did not trust humans or demons, or anyone else aside from her fellow Darts.

Life had taught her that even other angels could not be relied upon, not with one's life, nor with one's heart. But she didn't have to trust the human before her. In these instances, coin spoke louder than words.

"I may know someone who can help," the elderly woman said. The human had nut-brown skin, with eyes like upside-down crescents, and wrinkles from a life that had contained much laughter. But there was a fierce glitter in those brown eyes, one that spoke of keen intelligence and a little greed.

Greed Seraphina could work with.

They sat at a rickety table in the woman's little shop in Manhattan—its walls were covered in shelves filled with herbs and spices, roots and tisanes, and the welcoming scent of old books and patchouli permeated the air.

A cabinet of crystals and stones stood next to their table, partially hiding them from general view. A young woman with red hair served a few straggling customers, but part of her attention was fixed on Seraphina and the elderly woman, like she would rush to the human's defense if required.

Seraphina had no doubt that the grandmotherly figure needed no assistance, especially not from the likes of a younger female who appeared to have little power.

After all, this was a magic shop—*the* best magic shop in the country, according to her sources—and one frequented by humans and the supernatural alike. It was also horrendously expensive and had a select range of clients for certain, *special* services. If the store owner or her assistants took a dislike to someone, that someone forgot they'd ever entered the store...and sometimes the last week of their life.

Seraphina had little fear that memory-altering magic would work on her, but she wasn't about to take any chances. The woman before her was a Crone, one of the most powerful witches in the country, and Seraphina was fallen.

"You may know someone, or you do know someone?" Seraphina could usually charm even the most stoic out of their shell—it was her role in their organization, after all—but she did not have the patience for it, not today.

Not after everything had been thrown into chaos.

Azrael appears to be involved with a demon, and Zadkiel has been tortured by God-knows-who, then rescued by said demon...

Love, it appeared, could soften even the hardest of demon—and angel—hearts.

Then why hasn't it worked for me?

Enough! She did not believe in self-pity and there was work to be done.

Thankfully, there was *always* work to be done, now they lived in the Human Realm.

"What's got your panties in a knot?" the Crone asked, her voice dry and cracked with age.

"Who says I am even wearing panties?" Seraphina countered.

The old woman cackled and took a sip of what appeared to be green tea. Seraphina hadn't been offered any—she wouldn't have accepted it, anyway. Witches were crafty creatures and Seraphina didn't feel like being poisoned.

"You want a healer," the human said, "but you don't say what for. How can I be certain that I can provide such a service, when I don't know what you need, exactly?"

"The individual has been tortured. There is extensive damage to their anatomy. I need someone who can repair tissue and bone."

She wasn't about to let this woman know that the prospective patient was an angel. It was too risky—while angel feathers were prized by demons, witches coveted their blood, skin and hair for spells.

Intelligent eyes met Seraphina's as the woman played with her teacup. "It will be expensive."

"I will pay what it costs." She leaned forward. "Provided it *works*."

The Crone jabbed a finger at the table. "I can't guarantee anything without seeing what we have to work with. You will pay for the time, material and expertise."

"I will pay what is fair."

Witches were mercenaries. They would charge their own mothers if they thought it would benefit them. Seraphina couldn't let the Crone think she was desperate—even though she was—because the check might be something they couldn't pay.

Raze is very rich, though.

But Zadkiel's wings had been *ruined.*

He is the only one of us left with flight. He deserves a second chance.

Oh, many would say he should lose his wings as she had lost hers; after all, he had actually been present while the Heart was stolen. But she wasn't petty like that, and anyone could see the soldier had been through Hell and back. Also, he wasn't technically fallen, not yet. Not until the archangels removed his wings.

He, at least, had a chance at restoring his former life.

He might even be able to enter Heaven and plea for their cause.

No one has helped you yet.

Well, there had been the archangel Aurora's offer to Azrael; but Raze believed it was a poisoned chalice. Other than that, they had been largely left to their own devices, tasked with finding the three pieces—not just the one segment that had been held in the Inner Sanctum—of Heaven's Heart.

"I'll come and see this patient for myself," the Crone said and drained her green tea.

Seraphina clenched a fist in surprise. "You will?"

"Yes, it's not every day that a fallen angel walks into my humble store and asks me to heal someone." A sardonic smile graced the woman's wrinkled face. She turned partially toward the counter and yelled, "Rowan!"

How had she known what I was?

Most of the people Seraphina worked with for the Falling Star—the Darts' mercenary company—had no clue as to her species, just that she was powerful and trigger-happy with it.

The red-headed shop attendant abandoned wiping the counter down with a cloth and hurried over. "Yes, Gran?" Bright-green eyes surveyed Seraphina.

"We're closing up early," the Crone said. "Get your purse, we're going on a field trip."

CHAPTER 21

"Why is this whore not dead?" Lord Farcon demanded.

Peony raised her eyebrows. Did the Mortus only have two forms of insult for females? 'Bitch' and 'whore'?

It probably reflects how they view women.

"You question how my uncle would rule his kingdom?" Godric asked coolly.

The lordly demon took a deep breath and stepped back. "Apologies Your Highnesses, I became overwrought. The loss of my brother has been difficult to deal with."

When a human said those words, Peony knew it was because they grieved their loss, but she didn't think that was the case here. The demon seemed angry, if anything, without a touch of sadness in his expression.

"You have been quite vocal in your discontent about how the matter has been handled," King Alvin said.

Lord Farcon swallowed.

The guards stepped away from the demon.

"She," the Mortus shot a glance at Peony, "killed him."

"He was a willing participant in the experiment."

"She slashed his face open!"

Peony bit the inside of her cheek. Dru's claws were razor sharp—the damage would have been horrendous.

"Trifling wounds," the king said and waved a hand in the air dismissively.

The Mortus must heal fast.

Peony and Dru did, so it stood to reason their demon relatives would, too. It was good to know, since she would now be making her home amongst these people.

How long will it take me to work off my debt?

Although the better question was: would they let her?

"Untie her," King Alvin said, nodding at Peony.

"What?" Lord Farcon looked wildly around the room. "She's a murderer!"

He's afraid of Dru.

Emotions clashed within her: pride that her sister hadn't been broken by the Mortus, horror that she had killed her own kind so easily.

The Mortus are evil.

Yes, but everyone deserves a chance at life. It's what her mother had taught her and why she'd wanted to become a doctor. According to most demons and humans, Peony shouldn't have been allowed to live, because of her contaminated genetics. She wasn't about to judge someone else because of their species, no matter that she could feel their evil in her bones.

One of the guards stepped up behind her and untied the rope around her wrists. Slowly, so as not to startle anyone, she drew her arms around to her front and rubbed the abused flesh through her gloves. Pins and needles zinged through her hands and forearms as the blood rushed back through her veins.

"Touch him," King Alvin ordered her.

Peony stared at him. "It will kill him."

"It may not."

"What? Touch me? Her skin is not toxic." Confusion warred with the anger on Lord Farcon's face.

She clasped her hands together and shook her head. She was *not* a killer: she would not break her promise, not now. She wasn't like Dru. She *helped* people.

The king took a threatening step toward her. "I said, touch him!"

She had to think of a way out of this. "I'm a doctor, I took an oath!"

There. Since they were demons they might not know exactly what human oaths entailed. Vows were binding for most demons.

Godric frowned. "Do no harm, I think that's what human doctors must swear to."

Peony had never been so grateful to the media and its misrepresentation of Lasagna's Oath before.

"You *swore* this?" The king looked baffled. "But you're Mortus."

"Only half," Peony said quietly.

"Abomination," Lord Farcon spat.

The king stared at her for a few moments before nodding at Godric. As one, the guards on either side of her grabbed her arms, holding her in place while Godric clasped Lord Farcon's hand in a tight grip.

"Take off your glove," Godric ordered Farcon.

Peony shook her head, and tried to back away, but the guards' hold tightened. "No, don't do this."

She didn't want his death on her hands—she already had enough guilt to live with. *I should have taken Dru or*

Sylvester up on those advanced self-defense lessons. Metcalf had also offered, but his version of self-defense was a little too brutal for her liking.

Lord Farcon removed his glove slowly, and Godric dragged him forward by the arm. "Touch her."

"I really don't see the point in this," the demon argued.

"Prove your loyalty to the crown and touch her!" King Alvin roared.

Green skin paling, Lord Farcon extended a shaking hand. He paused just before touching her face, rage in his brown eyes, then drew his hand back. She heard the slap before the sharp stinging pain registered. Shutting her eyes against it, she licked her lip and tasted blood.

A scream tore through the air.

Forcing herself to watch, she saw Godric step away from the flailing Mortus demon. Lord Farcon hit the floor hard, where he convulsed for three heartbeats and went still.

She didn't need to check his pulse or airflow to know he was dead.

The urge to vomit was almost overpowering, but she swallowed back the bile. Her stomach already hurt enough.

He just...died.

She stared in shock at the deceased Mortus.

You didn't do this, this wasn't your fault.

No, it was the king's and Godric's.

Your vow is still unbroken.

Godric prodded the body with a toe. "The other one's skin didn't do this."

King Alvin stepped forward, examining the dead lord

with a critical eye. Then he focused on her. "All your skin is like this?"

Peony nodded, mute.

"We will have to work out what to do with you, then. For now, we cannot use you for breeding." He glowered. "I do not like having people who do not contribute living on my generosity."

Thank the gods.

She didn't want to become a broodmare—she didn't want to be used and impregnated. How could the females here stand it?

"If she is a healer, she might come in useful," Godric murmured.

"Put her in with the harem for now."

The harem?

Peony was led through a warren of tunnels and corridors until she reached two large bronze doors guarded by more cloaked Mortus demons.

Why wear cloaks inside?

She guessed she'd find out eventually.

Godric nodded at one of the guards, who executed a short bow then opened the right-hand door.

Peony wasn't sure what she expected inside, but this wasn't it. Light spilled from various lamps and torches, illuminating every corner of a large open area that stretched for about two hundred yards. It felt airy, despite the fact it was deep underground. Bright turquoise and carnelian tiles lined the floor, woven in intricate geometric patterns, and gold and silver divans and sofas punctuated the room. Expensive Turkish carpets were carefully placed under tables and chairs.

A woman appeared from a side corridor, her head downcast and shoulders slightly hunched. While the room looked like something from an ancient Near Eastern palace, the female Mortus was dressed in clothes better suited to Victorian England.

"Your Highness." She dropped into a deep curtsey.

Wow.

Having grown up in America, the whole concept of lords and ladies and servant obedience was a tad foreign to Peony. Her experience with it hadn't improved since her relocation to Tartarus, either. She rarely left the Halcyon Guild buildings, and it wasn't like their Hell-lord, Hades, made a habit of visiting his subjects. His ruling style was more iron-fist-when-needed.

Which seemed to suit the guild perfectly.

"Please show..." Godric turned to her with a frown. "What is your name?"

"You didn't read the paperwork?" Peony asked, and immediately wanted to slap her hands over her mouth. This was not Trick. She was no longer in the guild.

The female Mortus gasped.

Godric raised an eyebrow. "You are new, so I will be tolerant. But take note: most others would beat you for that."

Corporal punishment for sarcasm?

The Mortus were as bad as she'd feared.

That chill gaze settled on her. "So, one more time. What is your name?"

"Peony."

He gave her a gracious nod. "Please show Peony to

her room. Further instructions regarding her duties will be forthcoming."

"Yes, Your Highness."

Godric turned to leave, then paused. "If you cause these women any harm, my uncle will have you killed, and I won't stop him."

Peony felt like she'd been slapped again. "I am a *doctor*."

"You will have to forgive my skeptical nature. I met your sister, after all."

Then he was gone, and Peony was left with her suitcase, and the female Mortus' curious attention.

Chapter 22

Z sat in the mansion's library, the scent of old books comforting in a way he hadn't thought possible. He was upright, seated on a stool, with his damaged wings descending to just above floor level. In a brightly lit corner of the library, Raze was quietly going through papers scattered over a walnut desk.

He didn't know where Yael, Seraphina, Azrael and Dru were. Actually, he preferred not to think about what Azrael and Dru were up to; Dru looked too much like Peony, even if she did have a hard edge Peony lacked.

For the better.

As his eyes wandered around the library while his gut throbbed dully: worry for Peony trapped in the Mortus den; concern that his wings may still have to be removed; guilt that he still *had* wings when the others had lost theirs.

At least I don't have to worry about Trick.

Well, not right now.

Trick would come for him eventually, since he still considered Z to be his blood-bound slave. Despite the magical handprint that had appeared on Z's torso that afternoon—Trick's, no doubt—his slave master would remain clueless as to Z's whereabouts. Yael had explained that the mansion was warded to the eaves, so provided Z stayed inside the grounds, he would be invisible to most magical enquiries.

The other Darts had been so solicitous that Z had gone to bed early, unable to deal with their care. He'd spent the night asleep on the carpeted floor of an immense bedroom. Near waking, he had dreamed of endless clear gray.

Peony.

He had to get well so he could rescue her from the Mortus, then help find Dina and the Heart.

"You really believe this healer will be able to repair my wings?" Z asked Raze.

"I don't know," Raze replied. "Seraphina seems to think there is a chance, and she is usually quite cautious about these things."

Truth.

Z's eyes traced his fellow Dart's wingless outline.

Raze is fallen. Because of me.

"Don't pity me."

Z jerked at the dark-skinned angel's voice.

"Everything happens for a reason. I don't feel sorry for myself."

Truth.

"No?" Z would, if they were to trade places.

Skies, he *had.* And his wings had simply been injured.

A chuckle escaped Raze as he placed his paperwork on the desk and stood up. He came over to sit next to Z, eyes settling on the view over the library and the lush rose garden outside. The tall angel crossed an ankle over a knee. "Well, I don't feel sorry for myself anymore. The first few months were...hard."

This was the most candid Z had ever seen Raze; he was normally quiet as a tomb.

"You honestly think this is for the best?" Z asked, disbelieving.

"The archangels want us to find all three parts of Heaven's Heart. Heaven only held one previously. Perhaps this is our destiny, to restore the Heart to its former glory." Raze's expression was bland as he spoke, so Z couldn't determine his sincerity. There was no lie there, however.

The Darts had spent centuries serving Heaven, only to be stripped of their wings and discarded like broken toys. Even Z felt betrayed, and he had been the one responsible for their punishment. *How can Raze not hate me?*

Would he hate one of them, if their roles had been reversed?

He wasn't sure he could answer that.

Ever since he was a small child, he'd wanted to be a warrior angel. To have lost that chance because of someone else's mistake...it would be devastating.

But it wasn't your fault. No one even noticed the Infernus had broken into the Celestial City until they were in the Inner Sanctum.

But then Z had been useless in the fight, getting knocked out and kidnapped early into the altercation.

He was an embarrassment.

The door to the library swung open on silent hinges. Seraphina stepped into the room and then shut the door behind her. Her brown eyes were solemn, her face expressionless. "I have help with me."

Z nodded, not sure what else to say.

Raze studied her expression. "What is your concern?"

"They are human."

"What can a human do to help me?" Z wondered.

"Well," she elaborated, "they are witches."

"*Witches.*"

Technically human, the magic-users were largely ignored by angels and demons alike, because they rarely interfered with Heaven's or Hell's business. They were often nothing more than basic spell-casters, with limited powers.

"I don't see how a witch can help me," Z said. Peony had tried numerous medical approaches, and Sylvester had even used demon magic. A witch could surely do no more than that.

"This isn't just any witch," Seraphina said softly. "She is a Crone."

Z pondered the significance of that statement. "She's old?" he asked finally.

Seraphina looked nonplussed.

Raze chuckled. "In the witch hierarchy, you have Maiden, Mother and Crone. Or Master, Father and Crone. Not everyone progresses from one level to another, and there are only a handful of Crones in the country." Raze tilted his head to the side. "And you managed to find one?"

"Yes, she runs a store in Manhattan."

"A shop?" Raze shook his head. "It takes all types, I guess."

"Shall I bring her in?" Seraphina asked. "I will have her swear a blood oath for secrecy."

Both angels turned to Z.

They're waiting for me to decide.

He doubted that a human could do much for him, but this wasn't just about him anymore.

"Do it."

Seraphina turned on her heel and left, returning with an elderly woman by her side. Through the open door, Z spotted another human, this one with hair the color of fire. She peered inside, only to have the door swing shut on her.

A door no one had touched...

He turned curious eyes on the Crone.

"My granddaughter does not need to see this," the human said, her dark eyes serious as they took in Z's broken form. The witch turned to Seraphina, her mouth pursed in distaste. "You didn't say you had an unfallen angel here."

"No."

"You had me swear a blood oath without the full information. That's cheating." But something about the woman's expression said she admired the trickery.

Humans.

They had never made much sense to him, but he'd never questioned God's will—humans were his children just as much as the angels were, and thus deserved protection from evil, AKA demons.

He was coming to understand, however, that not all demons *were* evil. And that humans were...complicated.

A thin smile graced Seraphina's lips. "You wanted to work with a fallen angel—that was a risk you took."

The Crone gave a low laugh, then rubbed her hands together. "I assume you want me to look at this young one's wings?"

"Young one?" Z croaked. He was probably four times older than the witch.

"I've been around the block more than once, angel-boy. I know age when I sense it." She nodded at Raze. "He's old. You're not."

Raze's storm-gray eyes widened slightly, before he settled back in his chair with a half-smile on his face.

Maybe he really does think losing his wings is for the best.

Was it selfish of Z to want his fixed? Maybe he shouldn't have agreed to see the witch.

The woman approached Z on surprisingly agile limbs. "May I touch them?"

He took a deep breath and nodded.

Careful fingertips brushed over the wing's radius bone, before gliding down over the fine dusting of pin feathers. Instead of pain—which was the usual accompaniment to having his wings treated—she left nothing but a sense of coolness in her wake.

She tsked a few times before eventually stopping.

"His wings will eventually heal on their own," she said, stepping away.

Z half-turned in his chair to look at her. "How long?"

She tilted her head to the side, sizing him up. "Months for full recovery."

Truth.

"*Months?*"

"There is extensive damage, and your natural healing ability is hampered." Her dark eyes glittered with an emotion he couldn't decipher.

The Infernus had a lot to answer for. Whatever poison they'd dosed him with needed to be catalogued and destroyed, if it could cause this much damage to an angel.

"Can you fix them?" Raze asked, his voice calm as an undisturbed lake.

"Of course." The Crone grinned. "Although, it will cost you a pretty penny."

Z's gut clenched. "How much?"

Could the others afford his healing? The house was spectacular, with extensive grounds and expensive furnishings, but what if all the Darts' money was tied up in the property?

"We will pay the cost, as discussed," Seraphina interjected.

Z opened his mouth to interrupt, but the Crone slapped a hand on his shoulder.

"Let's get started, then," she said. "My name is Theodora. But you can call me Dora." Then she winked at him.

He froze, unsure what to do. Was the human *flirting* with him?

She rolled up her sleeves, revealing finely wrinkled deep-brown arms. "Hmph. Did you lose your sense of humor along with your wings?"

A choking sound emerged from Raze, and Seraphina covered a smirk with a hand.

Z regarded her seriously. "I'm not sure I had one to begin with...Dora."

The Crone cackled. "Well, there's a lot magic can do, but making you funny is beyond even my considerable abilities."

CHAPTER 23

The room assigned to Peony was tiny—it had a single bed, desk, chair, naked lightbulb, and a standalone closet. There was just enough room for her to walk around the bed without bashing her shins against the wooden furniture. It was depressing; even her dorm room at college had been bigger than this.

Peony stared at the bare stone walls, feeling like they were closing in on her: that she was trapped deep beneath the earth with no way out.

You are. You're in Hell.

She placed her suitcase on the desk and removed her computer, hugging it briefly to her chest. She turned it on and waited impatiently for it to load, then tried to connect to the Internet. Nothing. Peony checked her cell phone, but it didn't have reception either.

You shouldn't be surprised.

If there was Internet here, it probably wasn't available to the women. It would give them a way out, and it seemed the Mortus males liked their women trapped in a harem.

Somehow, she'd try to work out how to email. If she didn't get in touch with her mom soon, Selene would descend on the guild, and it would end badly—mostly for the guild. She closed the laptop and rubbed her forehead. Not only did she *need* to reach her mother, she also wanted to check in with Dru; to find out what had happened when she'd been here.

Why Dru had been here.

Tucking the laptop back into her suitcase, she sighed. A new life stretched in front of her, one that didn't appeal—trapped in a harem to an abusive king. She tapped her fingers on the lid of her case while she thought. Peony was most likely safe from rape, since her skin was toxic, but how was she to stand by and watch the other women get used?

I will help them.

How, she wasn't sure yet.

Peony rose from the spindly chair and turned to the bed. She may as well get some sleep. She tugged at the fingers of her gloves, then stopped. No. It was better to leave her skin covered. Just in case. She didn't need to be the cause of any more deaths.

She lay on the lumpy mattress, her body refusing to release the tension that had been riding her all afternoon. *Tomorrow,* she told herself; tomorrow she would work out what to do, how to fit into this new life.

Peony's eyes snapped open in the darkness. She didn't move, trying to catalogue every sound as her eyesight adjusted to the lack of light. She didn't know what had triggered her alertness, perhaps just the strange new room, but fear was blooming in the pit of her stomach now, blood rushing through her veins.

There was a whisper of sound, cloth against cloth, and the gentle exhalations of barely suppressed breathing.

Her heartbeat spiked.

I'm not alone.

Without thinking, Peony rolled off the right-hand side of the narrow bed, taking the sheets with her. There was a whooshing sound as she slammed into the legs of someone next to the bed.

Wrong way!

Tangled, confused, she thrashed in the sheets, biting back a scream as hot pain scored her right arm, leaving wetness in its wake.

Peony screamed, as loud as she could.

Hands groped for her mouth. Peony struggled desperately, so the seeking palms didn't touch the skin of her face.

"Damnit!"

"Hurry up!"

There were *two* of them?

The voices are female...

Hands jostled her through the sheets, and Peony fought harder than she ever had in her life. These Mortus were *strong*. Finally, she hooked a leg free from the sheets and kicked out, hearing a grunt in response.

"Just finish it!" one of the women hissed.

A second later, Peony's arms were pinned to the stone floor; she flailed out with her free leg, but the other Mortus avoided her attack. A glint of light on metal caught her eye...

Then electric illumination burst to life, blinding her.

"Damnit, my eyes!"

"What is going on here?" a new voice demanded, sharp enough to slice the air.

Peony tried to focus on the tableau above her. A Mortus demon with jet-black hair, her classically beautiful features twisted with anger, held her down on the ground. Another stood poised over her with a knife, rubbing her eyes.

"We were just tucking the new recruit into bed," the demon standing over her said, quickly shoving the blood-coated knife behind her back.

Craning her neck, Peony took in the newcomer. Taller than average, the female Mortus was a study in elegance. From the immaculately coiffed auburn hair, complete with thin strands of silver, to the stern gray eyes and slightly up-tilted chin, she radiated power and barely contained anger.

"With a knife?"

Peony's captor's hands tighten in response.

"What knife?" the brown-haired demon blurted.

Impatience coated each word. "The one behind your back."

"We thought she needed a bit of a lesson in how things are done around here."

"You do realize," the older demon said, stepping into the room and closing the door behind her, packing the tiny space to capacity, "that if you had succeeded in killing this half-breed abomination, your lives would have been forfeit?"

Half-breed abomination?

At least Peony knew that the woman harbored no love

for her.

This rescue wasn't for *her* sake.

The brown-haired Mortus lowered the blade. "The king cannot afford to lose any women in the harem."

The older Mortus tsked. "Do not presume to think on behalf of the king. People have a way of dying young when they do."

"Can I get up now?" Peony asked. She had the feeling she was going to survive the night, now that her attackers had been discovered.

Emotionless gray eyes focused on her. "Speak only when spoken to, abomination."

She bit her lip.

Lovely.

But she stayed where she was.

Peony supposed she had been lucky; she had avoided much of the racism toward cambions in the Human World and Hell. Her mom had never tolerated it, and Peony's abilities had been useful to the guild, so aside from the initial teething problems, the other Halcyon members had largely accepted her. It had probably helped that they'd already known Dru and Sylvester. You didn't go calling them 'abominations' unless you were prepared to wear a brand-new smile across your neck.

"You two will leave, and you will not speak of this mistake to anyone else."

The demon holding Peony loosened her grip. "But, Your Grace—"

"Do I make myself clear?"

The knife-wielding Mortus turned to the doorway. "She killed our brothers!"

"They volunteered their lives in order to establish

whether or not the cambions were suitable breeding material."

"Cambions?" Confusion and rage warred on the black-haired Mortus' face, and she stood up from where she had Peony pinned.

The other attacker frowned thunderously. "Milly, what are you *doing*?"

"Why did you say 'cambions', plural?" Milly asked.

"Because this one is the twin to the first abomination, who killed your older brother."

"But Jerald died today—"

"Yes, the king wished to have this cambion tested as well. It turns out that her skin is toxic to the touch. You are lucky you did not come into contact with her face."

Both of the assailants turned a paler shade of green.

"Jewel, Millicent, I understand wanting to avenge your siblings." Both Mortus women stood up straight, pride etched in their posture. "But there was no real loss there. Your brothers were nothing more than wastes of space."

The girls' expressions grew taut.

The eyes of the older Mortus glinted with something like amusement. "If you had succeeded in killing this abomination, the king would have taken that as a questioning of his judgement. Your family would have paid the price, and you would have been killed or demoted from the harem. Would you prefer to be passed around the commoners' ranks as nothing more than whores?"

"Aren't we nothing more than whores anyway?" Milly asked, bitterness saturating her voice.

Peony lay still on the floor, hoping the three of them

would forget she existed. This was awkward, and not just because Milly and Jewel had tried to murder her mere minutes ago.

The older woman stepped right up next to Peony like she wasn't there, and gripped Milly by the jaw. "Don't ever voice that sentiment again, girl, unless you want to die. I can protect you only so much."

"Why bother at all?" Jewel muttered.

"Don't make me question my choice. Go."

A few seconds of tense silence, and then Milly and Jewel squeezed around the older demon and out the door. That left Peony alone with a woman who hadn't hidden her disdain of her.

Eventually, the demon asked, "Why didn't you kill them?"

"I don't make a habit of killing people."

The woman raised an auburn eyebrow. "Your sister does, from what I hear."

"I am not Dru."

The demon turned and walked to the door. "You might want to take a few lessons from her, if you wish to survive here."

"I'm no killer."

"Then you are a fool."

The door shut behind her with a decisive click.

Better a fool than a murderer.

But why didn't those words provide the comfort they once did?

CHAPTER 24

While Z wasn't entirely convinced as to the Crone's—Dora's—sanity, she was efficient. Within moments of a second blood oath occurring, this one for the job itself, she had a bag set up on Raze's desk, and had withdrawn numerous glass bottles and sachets from it. There were some strange-colored powders and liquids among them, the sulfur-yellow one looking especially ominous.

"What's that?" Z asked, pointing.

Dora squinted at the bottle. It didn't appear to have a label. Was he going to be poisoned by accident? "Powdered dragon urine."

"Powdered *what*?"

The witch looked at him like he was dim-witted. "You never know when it will come in handy."

"But what does it *do*?"

She shrugged. "Lots of things."

"Dried dragon urine has been traditionally used by witches for the past two thousand years," Raze said, as if he were reciting from a book. "Originally believed to help cure urinary tract infections, it has since been used for a range of ailments, and is thought to be especially good for treating burns."

Dora glared. "Show off."

The corner of Raze's mouth quirked upward. "I did spend the first three hundred years of my life as a scholar."

Maybe he doesn't resent his punishment because he's already had to give up one dream.

What if being a soldier had *never* been Raze's dream?

No, that was silly. Who wouldn't want to serve Heaven and its armies? It's all Z had ever wanted, and only the best of the best had been assigned to the Darts. You couldn't be as good as Raze at fighting if you didn't love it.

"Now, I am going to make a poultice for your wings where they are still damaged. It will sting when I apply it."

"So do you plan on putting other kinds of urine on me?" There were a few other alarmingly colored liquids and powders on the desk.

Dora barked a laugh. "Do you realize that sounds like an invitation?"

He frowned. "For what?"

Dora looked over his shoulder at Seraphina and then Raze. "If you don't know, and those two aren't saying, I am not going to be the one to explain it."

The other angels kept quiet.

The witch turned away and began mixing ingredients, muttering under her breath the whole time. Z kept a careful eye on the proceedings, just to make sure the dragon pee stayed where it was.

"Are you sure about this?" he asked Seraphina

quietly.

She nodded. "She is one of the most powerful witches in the country. Everywhere I asked, it was Theodora Broome that was recommended."

Broome?

Isn't that a bit cliched?

Then again, most human surnames found their origins in ancestral careers.

Dora turned, a greenish pile of goop in her left hand. "I am not one of the most powerful witches in the country." She gave Seraphina a stern look. "I am *the* most powerful witch in all of the Americas."

Truth.

And apparently her hearing was much better than her age would suggest.

"Can't you just use magic, then?" Z asked her.

Dora hmphed and began slathering the mixture on the bones of his wings. "I could, but it would take a lot more power than necessary, and the spell would take longer to be effective. It would also drain you more, since I'd need to use your body's own healing ability to do a lot of the work. Doing it this way, I can use the strong magic for the parts that need it."

He wasn't sure he agreed with her logic, but then he didn't know much about human magic. "What's the poultice do?" he asked.

"It will draw out any infection or poison. Now, I'm not here to conduct a lesson. Take your shirt off."

Z paused for a moment, then pulled the black T-shirt over his head, careful not to disturb the poultice. He'd never worn clothing like it before, but it—and the trousers—had been donated by Azrael. Yael had said the other fallen angels' clothing was too expensive to be cut up to allow for wing-slits.

Dora shook her head sadly. "What a waste."

"What is?" he asked.

"The first time I lay eyes on a half-naked angel and his body is skin and bone. There goes that fantasy."

Z preferred to not think about her statement in any great detail.

The Crone laid her hands on his shoulders, and warmth bloomed within him, racing through his veins. It wasn't like the healing generated by Peony's demon friend — this was purer, somehow, more like his own life-force.

How is she doing this?

"With skill and power," Dora said, answering his thought. "Now stop thinking so hard, you're distracting me."

Alarm raced through him at the realization she could read his mind, and he felt more than heard her mirth.

"Your secrets are safe with me," she said softly, "provided you don't concentrate on them during the healing."

Z took several deep breaths, using a meditation technique he'd been taught during his early years in warrior training. The goal wasn't to think of nothing, but to find a peaceful part of his mind and focus on a single thought: a skill he wanted to learn, a book he'd been reading or, in this case, saving Peony.

"Better," the witch mumbled.

The heat emanating from her hands ramped up, to the point where he began to sweat. Little zaps of lightning shot through his nervous system, distracting him from the meditation technique.

Dora removed her hands from his shoulders, and he turned to face her. Her wrinkled face was drawn slightly, and her breath wheezed. "I need more power."

"We cannot transfer our magic to your kind—" Seraphina began.

"I don't need *your* power." She plucked a cell phone from her pocket and rapidly typed something into the screen. "I'll just borrow some from my granddaughter."

"You can do that?" Raze tilted his head to the side. His fingers fluttered, as if searching for a writing instrument to document the answer.

"With a conduit, yes. Not with just anyone. Rowan is one of the strongest born in three generations."

There was pride in that statement, and something else, something melancholy and perhaps a little bitter. But their family drama was not Z's issue. He already felt stronger, although his head was pounding and he was thirsty, like he'd been walking in a desert for months without water.

"Can I have a drink?" he asked.

Dora stared at him for a few moments, her dark eyes serious. "Yes, a few sips. Water only."

Seraphina poured a glass and handed it to him silently. He took three mouthfuls then passed it back, Dora's eyes tracking his every movement to ensure that he had obeyed her instructions. He wasn't sure what a little bit of extra water would do to the spell casting, but he didn't understand human magic, so he wasn't about to mess with her request.

The Crone's phone chimed, the sound like a shop's bell.

Then her hands were back on his shoulders, and the rush of power hit him, hard. The steady warmth was now a stream of lava, and his head throbbed in time with his heartbeat. A strange burning sensation started in his gut, then spread throughout his body. The electrical zaps had transformed into a maelstrom of lightning, but he didn't utter a sound.

The others would stop Dora if they thought he was in pain.

The healing seemed to go on forever, but it may have just been moments. Finally, Dora's hands left his shoulders, and he doubled over, breathing heavily, sweat slicking his skin. The lingering ache made him long for Peony's treatments—and he'd thought *her* attentions were painful.

Dora thumped down into a chair next to him. Flicking a glance her way, Z took in her pinched features and weary expression.

"A week," she croaked.

Seraphina quickly handed the Crone a glass of water. Dora gulped the liquid, then held the glass up and wiggled it in the air. "More, please."

The angel obeyed and Dora drained the second glassful.

"What about a week?" Raze asked eventually.

"I give it a week and he will return to full health."

A week.

It was almost too much to believe.

The door to the library was thrown open then, and Yael stood on the threshold, one hand gripped around the upper arm of the red-headed human woman Dora had left outside. He was dressed in a suit, but Z could see at least one knife hilt and knew that there would be another two or three stashed on his person, plus a garrote. That was his favorite weapon.

The redhead was wild-eyed, her hair a curling nimbus around her face. Raze and Seraphina quickly stepped in front of Z, shielding him from her view.

Yael's aquiline features were drawn in barely concealed irritation. "I found this human loitering around." Then he spotted Dora. "What is *that* doing here?"

The sparkle that had been present in Dora's eyes throughout most of the afternoon vanished. "I am not a '*that*'."

Yael yelped and let go of the young woman. Z assumed Dora had zapped him with her magic.

"They are here at our invitation," Raze said carefully. "Please leave the human alone."

Azrael and Dru appeared behind Yael then, then pushed past him into the room. Dru eyed the red-haired woman, then Dora.

"Yael, I know your personality sucks, but even you know that manhandling a woman is a bad idea, right?" Dru's voice rang through the room, forcing a chuckle even from Z. "I catch you doing it again and you'll lose the hand."

Yael glowered at her.

There seemed to be no love lost there.

"Rowan, love, did he hurt you?" Dora called out.

The redhead stopped rubbing her arm. "Not really."

Dora stood, taking a shaky breath. She clapped a hand on Z's naked shoulder. "Your wings will grow back," she said quietly. "Seraphina agreed to fair payment: know that as part of the payment, I want a favor granted to me in the future."

He held her dark gaze. "Deal."

And a tingle spread through him as the agreement was sealed, this magic older than time itself.

CHAPTER 25

Peony kept largely to her room and the two communal chambers where she was allowed access: the general rest area and the dining hall. No one spoke to her, and when she walked into a room, the reception was almost physically chilly. Standing in the entrance to the dining hall, she looked over the forty or so women assembled there. They were all dressed in Victorian-era gowns in a range of colors from the palest pink to deep sunset orange, with their hair upswept into fancy styles that Peony imagined took hours to complete.

She felt out of place here: disconnected. She didn't share the olive-green complexion of the others and she was the only one to have a shock of white hair; most of the women had locks that ranged from brown to black.

She was also conscious of her jeans and woolen sweater that Selene had knitted for her one Christmas. It was gaudy, in reds and yellows and greens, but it was warm and it wasn't scrubs, which comprised most of her wardrobe. So far, there had been no use for her medical talents here. None of the female Mortus spoke to her, beyond the bare minimum required, and when she tried to engage one in conversation, the other demon always had somewhere else to be.

Sighing, she took an empty seat at the far end of one of the tables and smiled at the male servant who approached her with a bowl of soup. He wore a crisp white shirt, complete with black cravat and trousers, and shiny boots. The demon stumbled slightly, then righted himself and placed the bowl in the empty place in front of her. Not a single drop of soup was spilled on the white linen tablecloth, despite his brief unsteadiness. Peony wasn't sure what the dish was made of, and she wasn't going to ask. The Mortus lived in Inferno; the flora and fauna would be quite different to the Human Realm and Tartarus. She was better off not knowing the dish's ingredients, otherwise she might not keep her food down.

"Don't smile at the servants."

Peony looked over her shoulder at the speaker. It was a younger female Mortus, with blonde hair that shone with red-gold highlights. It was strikingly different in the sea of black and browns, although not as distinctive as Peony's.

"Sorry?" She wasn't sure she understood the statement. Was it wrong to be polite?

You are in the den of the Mortus, some of the most feared demons in all three circles of the underworld. Of course it's wrong.

"Don't smile at them." The blonde had eyes that reminded Peony of violets. "They are already castrated — if you smile and they return any kind of sentiment, they will be punished. Ignore them."

Castrated.

She looked anew at the male servants floating elegantly around the room, pouring drinks, serving appetizers and entrees.

Why did they have to be mutilated for that?

"The harem is for the king and noblemen only," the blonde explained, having interpreted Peony's shocked expression. "No one else may procreate with us."

There was a slap, and Peony stared at the Mortus next to the blonde. The unfamiliar dark-haired demon had hit the blonde on the exposed skin of her arm, leaving a purple handprint.

"You do not speak to the abomination."

The blonde lowered her chin, almost to her chest, but did not reply.

Then the dark-haired demon glowered at Peony. "Don't speak to us."

Peony hadn't started the conversation—the blonde had only tried to be helpful, for the servant's sake—but she wasn't about to point that out. She wasn't going to get the blonde into more trouble.

Instead of replying, she spooned a mouthful of soup and focused on eating. It had a strange aftertaste, but wasn't entirely unpleasant. It was followed by meat and what she assumed were vegetables, and a dessert she didn't want—it had a little too much resemblance to pus.

When she stood, half of the eyes in the dining hall focused on her. Some were curious, but most were angry.

Thanks, Dru.

Although, even the Mortus female who'd saved her on her first night in the harem hadn't thought that Dru's victim—or Peony's—was worthy of life.

As Peony left the dining room and walked into the communal area, she spotted a woman coming through a door to the far right, away from the main double doors. She had jet-black hair and wore nothing but a dark-red silk nightgown that had been badly ripped. Her face was a mottled collection of bruises as she turned a blind gaze on the room. Then she tottered unsteadily and collapsed.

Peony rushed forward. She reached the demon's side seconds after she fell, and quickly checked her airways and heartbeat, before rolling her into the recovery position. Peony was strong, but she didn't want to move the demon on her own—this close, she realized it wasn't the nightgown itself that was red; it was stained with blood.

The demon's face was largely unrecognizable; a broken nose had resulted in two black eyes, and her lip was split and oozing blood. Peony ran her hands over her, trying to catalogue the wounds. The demon's skull reminded her of Z's.

Not again.

Why must people hurt each other?

"What did you do?"

Peony snapped her head up to look into the clear gray gaze of the demon who'd saved her life two nights ago.

"Why do you assume I did anything?" Peony asked, then scowled. That clearly was *not* the best response she could have provided. "She came in looking like this." She pointed at the silver-painted door behind her.

"I see." There was no emotion in the older demon's face.

The woman barked out a series of orders, and within a minute, a hospital gurney was brought for the fallen demon.

They have medical facilities here?

The injured woman was loaded carefully onto the trolley by three Mortus females who had been in the dining room minutes earlier, and then they were wheeling her away. Peony followed, wishing she'd spent more time cataloguing the girl's injuries.

"Why are you still here?" the older demon asked, glaring at Peony over the gurney.

"I'm a doctor, I can help."

A dismissive wave was her response, but Peony wasn't asked to leave.

Soon, they reached a stone-walled room, kept warm by a small brazier in one corner. The smell of something like antiseptic hung in the air, and a steel table was set in the middle of the room, reminding Peony of a surgical theatre. A floor-to-ceiling glass cabinet lined the rear wall, full of jars and bags and herbs that she doubted she could name.

It's some kind of clinic.

Not like the clinic she'd run, but probably one more suited to Hell.

The injured demon was transferred to the steel table, and then the gray-eyed Mortus placed her hand on the girl's shoulder. The other women dispersed, leaving only one behind—the blonde from dinner.

Peony took stock, then made for the door.

The older woman glanced up. "Where are you going? I thought you could help." Mockery dripped from her words.

"I need to get my medical bag." Then Peony was out the door, running back to her room. Her kit had taken up half the space in her suitcase, but she was glad she had brought it.

The total trip only took a few minutes, but she was worried it might be a few minutes too long, considering the demon had a fractured skull and had been bleeding from a variety of wounds.

She hurried back into the room, placed her kit on the gurney and opened it. Spotting a sink in the corner, she washed her hands and replaced her gloves with a disposable latex pair. Then she was back beside the patient.

The swelling around her nose had already begun to recede, as had the bruising around her eyes.

She's a fast healer.

That was a boon.

"What is your name?" Peony asked the older demon.

The blonde gasped from her position near the brazier, where she was soaking cloths in hot water. Had Peony just committed some extreme social faux pas?

The woman let out a low chuckle, but it held no amusement. "You can call me Your Grace."

Peony glanced up from where she was examining the injured demon's throat. Bruising the size and shape of hands marred the olive-green skin. "That's your name?"

"It's a title," the blonde demon explained. "Lady Eramine is the Duchess of Windmere. You address her using her title."

The duchess glared at the blonde, who promptly closed her mouth and returned to soaking cloths.

Peony couldn't help but like the chatty young demon—she didn't feel evil, like Godric or his uncle. *The Mortus are just like the members of the Halcyon Guild.*

Individual, with varying degrees of darkness on their souls.

Peony stepped around the end of the metal table and almost slipped in a pool of fresh blood. Hurriedly, she cut the nightgown away and swore. "What the Hell did they do to her?"

Rape. Rape is what happened.

If Peony had seen this in the ER and told Selene about it, the attacker would never have lived to be reported to the human police. Her mom may not like demons or angels overly much, but she hated rapists even more.

Peony propped the demon's legs wide and swore again at the damage. She then pressed a cloth between the Mortus' thighs to stem the flow of blood. "Please, hold this here," she said to the blonde.

Ripping off her gloves, she rifled through her kit and grabbed the gear she needed, then put a new set of gloves on and got to work.

"What are you doing?" the blonde asked.

"She has a third-degree tear," Peony explained. "Something you would normally see in childbirth." But that had clearly not been the cause of this injury. "I am going to stitch it back together."

Which she did, as quickly as she could, worried about the blood loss. She muttered while she worked, mostly curses at the disgusting asshole who had hurt this Mortus woman. Even demon species that healed quickly could die if they bled out too fast for their body to repair.

With the sutures in, Peony made another thorough assessment of the demon's injuries, pausing when she reached the girl's head.

The injured demon was recognizable now the bruising

and swelling to her face had reduced.

It was Milly.

Peony's gaze snapped to Lady Eramine's.

"She is a very fast healer..." Peony muttered. She wondered if the stitches had been a good idea. They would dissolve, but only in two to three days.

She noticed Milly's broken nose was also repaired, although no one had reset the bone—unless it had been done while she was retrieving her medical kit. Her fingers felt Milly's scalp—no fracture.

"We Mortus heal quickly," the duchess said, her face drawn. "But not that quickly."

"Then how is she—?"

"I am a natural healer."

Peony frowned. "I'd never heard of the Mortus having that ability."

"My mother was Pollus. I was born Mortus, but I had some of her traits."

When demons bred with other demons, one species always bred true. But it appeared that abilities from the other race were also inherited.

Behind Lady Eramine, Peony could see the blonde demon's mouth hanging open. Apparently, this was something of a revelation. And it explained a lot: Sylvester was a Pollus cambion, and he was able to heal most injuries without medical intervention.

"Why didn't you stop her bleeding?" Peony asked into the quiet that had descended.

"My ability fixes the most severe injuries first. She had a fractured skull and fractured cervical vertebrae."

"From being beaten and choked."

The duchess tilted her head in acknowledgement.

"How can you stand this?" Peony asked, ripping off her gloves and throwing them in the trash.

There was no response, Lady Eramine's eyes having gone stone cold at the question.

The blonde bit her lip, then said quietly, "Because it is the way things are."

Not if I can help it.

CHAPTER 26

The door to the main hall in the guild slammed open. Trick's attention was snared, but he kept his usual relaxed pose: one leg thrown over the arm of his throne, and a fist propping his chin up. Charcoal-colored smoke curled around the doorway, indicating that someone had teleported here, using a spell rather than an innate ability.

There weren't many people who would dare to burst into the Halcyon Guild, and he quickly ran through the list in his mind: Hades; Hades' personal assistant, Asha Himm; and Dru. None of those folks needed a spell to teleport—well, Dru did, but she'd be likely to use a Devilsgate, since that was cheaper. That said, she was rich now after cashing in her loot from the Set's castle, so who knew?

Two people stepped into the hall, and Trick fought the urge to straighten to immediate attention. With deep green eyes, and hair the color of Tartarus' sky at midnight, the woman was so beautiful she made supermodels look ugly. But it wasn't her physical appearance that caught him; it was her power.

She was a Nephilim.

What the Hell—?

"*Where is she?*" the woman demanded. Her green eyes were wild, and her cherry-red mouth was pressed into a thin line of rage.

There was a man behind her, but Trick couldn't make out his features. He could discern a stylish designer suit, complete with mandarin collar, but couldn't tell the man's skin tone or hair color.

A sorcerer. And a powerful one at that.

The other occupants of the hall had frozen at the newcomers' arrival, and no one moved as the Nephilim stepped further into the room, her furious stare locked on Trick.

"*Where. Is. She?*"

Slowly, so as to appear like he didn't have a care in Tartarus, he swung his leg to the front of the chair, and leaned forward, elbows on his knees. "Where is who?"

Trick had plenty of female assassins, any one of them might have irritated this powerful woman. Hell, Dru might have pissed her off accidentally; her people skills were that good.

Trick fought to keep the frown from his face—he didn't want to think about Dru, or the fact that she'd left him. Left the guild.

Instead, he focused on this Nephilim, the rarest species of the rare. Half-demon, half-angel, they were slaughtered by Heaven's armies whenever they were found. Demons didn't tend to treat them much better: too powerful to let live, too alluring to kill.

"Peony."

"You're looking for a flower?"

Someone snorted at his side and he flicked a glance at Sylvester, who glared at him with the full force of his disapproval. It turned out that most of the guild hadn't approved of Trick selling Peony to the Mortus—he had had no idea how well-liked the cambion had been. It was an inexcusable error on his part, but he had had little choice. He'd do it again, even if it had cost him two free guild members already.

"I am looking for my *daughter*."

Oh, shit.

This was bad, this was so bad. Why hadn't Peony ever mentioned that her mother was a freaking Nephilim?

Sylvester cleared his throat, and Trick shot him a look that clearly said to shut the Hell up.

Sylvester ignored him. "She's with the Mortus."

Rage pulsed over the woman's features, and every light in the room shorted out, electrical sparks flying over the occupants.

"She's *what*?"

Chapter 27

Two days had passed since the healing, and Z felt like he had spent most of it eating and sleeping. Truly, he doubted he'd ever consumed so much food before in his life. And it had all been so different to Heaven's meals. It turned out that angels were vegans, not that he'd ever known there was a term for it, but here there were things like bacon and eggs, and sausages, and steak.

And he really liked the taste of them.

He supposed he should feel guilty, but he didn't.

He lay on the plush, cream-colored carpet of his room—it had basically become his bed—and stretched out his arms and wings then froze. Looking over his shoulder, he saw soft plumage arching over his back and onto the floor.

His wings had grown back.

Completely.

Wonder and joy bubbled through him at the realization: he was whole again.

No more would he be a burden on the Darts—he could save Peony, then with her help, they could use Odin's

Orb to find Dina and the remaining pieces of the Heart. After that, he would no longer be ashamed of his failure. And he would have repaid Peony for her care.

You can show her the real you.

Not the sick, weak version of himself that she'd been exposed to. He would prove to her that he was a grown male angel, and someone worthy of the respect and kindness she'd already shown him.

Stretching a wing over his head, he stroked the soft feathers, then paused, his hand hanging in mid-air.

They were pure white.

Not a single strand of silver was to be found.

I am no longer warrior class.

His sense of happiness burst, and his eyes burned. So quickly his elation had soured. *This* was his punishment. He was no longer a warrior of Heaven—he was just a regular angel.

Maybe this is the price you had to pay for your failure, and for using human and demon magic to cure your injuries.

There was a knock; Azrael stood in the doorway, his dark hair jaw-length and framing his face. Before their fall, Azrael had never had a haircut that wasn't military standard. Behind him, Dru appeared, her face so painfully familiar and yet so utterly alien that it jarred him back to reality.

You are still an angel. Act like it.

He shoved himself to his knees, his wings a graceful sweep behind him.

Lucky I don't sleep naked. He used to, back in Heaven, but he hadn't liked the idea of dropping his trousers in Hell, nor here.

"You're looking much better," Azrael said, coming

into the room.

Dru stared from the doorway, a thoughtful look on her face. "You're skinny enough that Opal would approve of your physique. You need to eat more."

If he ate more, he'd need to buy shares in a supermarket chain.

"Who is this Opal?" he asked. Peony had mentioned her as well.

"She's a Radiato demon. They think the skeletal look is hawt."

He looked down at himself, at his prominent ribs and concave stomach. "I will improve."

"Yes, but how quickly?" Dru asked. She was studying him like he was a bug on a specimen tray.

He narrowed his eyes. "What aren't you telling me?"

Dru closed the door behind her. "We need to go after Peony ASAP. I am worried the longer she's there, the worse condition she will be in when she's found."

Z stood and walked over to his closet, where he grabbed another of Azrael's modified shirts and shrugged it on. The garment hung loosely on his frame, whereas once the two angels had been of similar musculature. He looped a belt around his waist as well, so that his trousers didn't fall off his hips.

"I am not sure I will be able to do much fighting, to be honest," Z admitted. Even though he had his wings back, he was weak as a newborn babe. "One more day?"

Not that he was sure an extra day would make a huge amount of difference, but he was recovering faster than he'd anticipated, courtesy of Dora's healing.

"We need a plan, anyway," Dru said.

Azrael quirked an eyebrow. "You said plans are for

wimps."

"*Your* plans are for wimps. My plans rock. That's how we managed to find Odin's Orb."

Azrael coughed. "*Your* plan?"

"Well, it certainly wasn't Yael's."

"On that, we agree."

A heated look passed between the pair, and then they focused on Z. He swallowed.

"Come and get some breakfast," Dru said, then left Azrael and Z alone.

Clear blue eyes locked on the sweep of white behind Z's shoulders. "I'm sorry."

Z choked back an involuntary sob. He would not cry; this was his punishment. He was far better off than Azrael; to act upset would only rub salt in his friend's wound.

"I deserve nothing less," Z said, and looked at the ground.

Azrael clapped him on the shoulder. "Don't blame yourself. You were on guard with Dina, who is like a battalion of angels all on her own. The fact both of you got taken—it meant that it was one Hell of an attack."

Z raised his eyes to meet Azrael's. "Being here has changed you," he blurted.

He nodded. "That and meeting Dru. She's so alive—accepts who she is utterly: where's she's been, what she's done. It makes you realize that pity won't get you anywhere. I still think those archangels are asses for what they did to us, but provided you can stay free and keep your wings, that will keep me happy."

Azrael had changed more than Z realized, to want to thumb his nose at the most powerful angels among their kind.

"Come on," the dark-haired angel said. "Let's go downstairs."

They were in the library again, this time all of them together. Yael was still fuming over discovering a human at their mansion, despite the blood oaths that had been sworn. Dru had told him to go shove his head up his butt, and things had devolved into an argument Z had decided to ignore. The two of them appeared to have a hate-hate relationship, and he didn't want to get involved in it.

"Want some whiskey?" Raze asked.

Z turned to the angel and stared at the amber liquid partially filling a cut-crystal class. He shook his head, the smell strong enough to make his stomach churn.

There was a sound of wood slamming into plaster, a tense second of silence, and then everyone launched into action, bolting from the room. Lurching upright, Z followed as the others sprinted into the foyer.

There, standing in the broken doorway, was a woman that made his every sense snap to life.

He didn't know what she was, just that she was lethal.

A magical wind whipped her hair around her face, and her green eyes burned with an intensity that was almost frightening. Behind her, a man lingered in the shadows of the twilight evening, the fine tailoring of his suit all that was visible.

The foyer smelled of green fields and woodsmoke.

Dru skidded to a halt on the marble floor, a knife in each hand. "*Selene?*"

Z eyed the shocked expression on Dru's face, and then the cold anger etched on the newcomer's.

Selene took a step forward. "Where is she?"

Yael slid closer to the strange demon, only to be whipped back against a wall by an invisible hand. He grunted at the impact, and strained, but could not move. The gun in his hand dropped to the floor with a clatter.

The others stood at the ready, but no one moved.

"Where is Peony?" Dru asked, her voice almost hesitant.

Why was this fearsome creature asking after his healer?

Z didn't like this at all. Peony would never be able to protect herself from such an individual—and he wasn't strong enough to do so, either. May never have been, even when he'd been at full power.

"Yes. That guild leader of yours told me he had sold her to the Mortus, but that is not possible." Another gliding step forward. "Is it?"

Dru winced and lowered her blades. "Trick isn't my leader anymore, and he did do it."

Crystal burst in the chandelier above them, raining glittering shards down on their faces, shoulders and chests. He could feel cuts across his exposed skin. Light dimmed in the room, only to be replaced by glowing orbs of magical fire.

He had to protect Peony from this woman.

"How could you let this happen? She joined the guild because of you. You promised me you would protect her!" Rage filled the room, until it was an almost physical presence.

"I was on a mission—which went wrong. I had

managed to get enough treasure to buy our freedom, but by the time I returned, the Mortus had requested Peony, and Trick had sold her." Fury met fury as Dru stared at Selene.

Then suddenly, the room calmed, and Selene stood there, hands open, tears tracking down her cheeks. "My daughter is in the hands of the Mortus."

Her daughter?

Z felt as if he had been punched in the gut. This woman was Peony's mother? As powerful as she was, there would be no need for Z to save his healer.

Every instinct in him protested at the idea.

No.

Peony was his to save.

The shadowed man strode into the room and laid a comforting hand on Selene's shoulder. "We can go after her."

Selene placed her hand over the shadow man's. "I can't go to Inferno."

The stranger's face came into view briefly, and Dru gasped. Azrael cursed.

"You're meant to be dead!" Yael growled. "I cut your fucking head off."

The shadow man was tall, with dark-brown skin and eyes that glittered like citrines. Desert winds and the scent of sand reached Z, reminding him of ancient worlds long forgotten.

He's a sorcerer.

"I haven't been decapitated recently, I can assure you." His accent was clipped, like English was his hundredth language.

"Recently?" Seraphina asked.

That glittering yellow gaze rested on the dark-skinned angel. "It's happened before once or twice."

And yet the demon lived.

"You mean you survived?" Yael demanded.

"You must be thinking of my brother, Set. I heard that he recently lost his head over a few trinkets." He chuckled darkly.

Z was sluggish, had no idea what was going on. Wait. Set? As in, the Egyptian god? That meant that the man before them was...

"*You're* Osiris?" Raze asked, one dark eyebrow arched.

The man gave a regal tilt of the head. "In the flesh."

They were standing before a god—well, a deposed one, but a god nonetheless. As far as Z had been aware, most of them had been destroyed during the Great Culling. A few famous deities had survived, like Hades and Kali, both incredibly hard to slay.

"Enough!" Selene spat. "We must rescue Peony. Now."

"We were planning on going tomorrow."

Selene frowned. "Tomorrow may be too late."

"Why?" Azrael asked.

"Because they can't learn who her father is, or they'll kill her."

CHAPTER 28

Godric stood in the doorway of Peony's room. "Come, walk with me."

She didn't want to leave the confines of her space, to have to deal with the reality of a place where brutal rape was so commonplace that a healer had been permanently assigned to the harem. And where the women of the harem had become accustomed to it.

"I would prefer not to," she replied wearily.

She'd spent the night monitoring Milly, despite Lady Eramine saying it was unnecessary. But she hadn't wanted to leave the demon alone, in case whoever had raped her came back for seconds.

And what would you have done? Hit him over the head with your medical bag?

She could have touched him. Just a single delicate stroke of her finger over his exposed skin, and he would have died in brutal agony. Partial repayment for what he had done to that girl. But Peony wasn't a murderer, couldn't break her oath. And nothing could ever really make up for what had been done to Milly.

"It wasn't an invitation." Godric shot her a look that was hard to decipher, and she shivered at his emotionlessness.

"Fine." Peony stood, feeling old and worn in her hospital scrubs. She'd decided her jeans and sweater combination were ill-suited to her new home—it was better to be prepared in a place like this, rather than not.

Godric exited the room, holding the door open for her. She walked by him, wondering why her skin didn't itch the way it did around his uncle.

They're both evil. They both allow these atrocities to occur.

He was just as bad, yet her instincts said he was no direct threat to her.

"Let's go." He shut the door, then strode away, toward the communal area.

"I cannot have sex with you," Peony blurted. "If what you do around here can even be called sex."

The demon stopped short. "Excuse me?"

Peony planted her feet. "If you try to have sex with me, you will die."

Godric scrunched his face up, then laughed. "I do not want to fuck you."

Something like embarrassment hummed through her. "I don't understand."

"I want to show you something." He held up a gloveless hand. "And no, it's not my cock."

Closing her jaw, because it had begun to hang open at some point, she followed him silently through the communal area and out the double doors into the hall.

He gave her a sideways look. "Follow me, and do not talk to anyone."

She nodded, not understanding what was happening,

but prepared to fight for her life if need be.

But I don't feel scared.

She couldn't explain it. It wasn't that she trusted Godric—Hell, no—but she didn't feel in danger from him. More, she felt like she *entertained* him somehow.

They walked in silence, passing numerous Mortus men who stared at her with a mixture of lust, hatred and rage. She followed Godric's instructions, and kept her eyes locked firmly on the stone floor in front of her, speaking to no one.

The stares made her feel dirty somehow, and in need of a shower.

As they continued through the halls, Peony wondered how she could ask about the treatment of the females in the harem. Godric was royalty; surely he could do something to stop it?

He probably treats women the same way, though.

Hell, he might have been the one responsible.

Something in her rejected that thought, even though she had no reason to do so.

He's evil, you can feel it as a pulse against your skin.

Eventually, they stopped in a corridor empty of people. Peony looked up at the walls, which were engraved with the same strange script she had seen on her first day in the Mortus den.

Godric stood at her elbow, his expression serious and lacking the mocking quality she had come to associate with it. "Can you read it?"

She looked at him, surprised. "You want me to read *that*?"

"You tried to before."

With her worry over Milly, she'd forgotten how some

of the text on the walls had swum together to form words. "I don't know the language."

He leaned forward, his eyes intense. "Just try."

For some reason, that look reminded her of Dru—they were both forceful to the point of zealousness.

"Why?"

"I'm curious."

"If I do this, what will you do for me?" Peony asked.

He barked out a surprised laugh. "I don't have to do anything for you. You're our prisoner, in case you had forgotten. One my uncle wants to kill."

She glared. "Let him try."

Godric reached out and took hold of her arm, hand touching only her sleeve. "Don't challenge him. He'll kill you in your sleep."

She rolled her eyes. "Someone already tried that."

"What?" He let go of her arm.

"They failed, in case you didn't realize."

"Who?"

Peony shrugged. "It doesn't matter. Lady Eramine stopped it."

"Lady Era—wait, she *stopped* it?"

"Why, do you think she was the mastermind behind it?"

"I wouldn't put it past her," Godric muttered. "Grandmother is very sneaky. And she hates cambions with a passion."

Peony stood stock still. "She's your *grandmother*?"

"And the king's mother."

So, Lady Eramine was connected at the highest levels, and she hadn't put a stop to the horrors, either. Why could no one see this was *wrong*?

Because they're evil.

But even then, there were boundaries, surely. Especially with your own kind...

"Are you going to just stand there looking dumbstruck? Or are you going to read?" Godric said, interrupting her thoughts.

"Fine."

Peony had never been very good at languages. Her skills had been in biology, chemistry and mathematics, and, later, medicine. She hadn't had time to learn another language once she'd started medical school. Still, she stared at the strange text, to humor the demon beside her. Maybe, if he thought she was making an effort, she could ingratiate herself, and then try to request help for Milly.

You're a dolt.

No, she was an optimist.

Ignoring her inner voice, she focused on the circular text, frowning as some words began to make sense. Not all of them, but enough that she could focus on different passages on the wall.

'The children of Satan...'

'Death to our enemies...'

'My brethren in the sky do not understand...'

'Love and hate are just two sides of the same emotion...'

'The day will come when the king is overthrown...'

"What is this?" Peony whispered, overwhelmed by the strange language. How could she even understand it? "Where does it start?"

"It's everywhere," Godric said, his voice quiet. "It was carved into the walls long ago—supposedly by our female ancestor."

"Female ancestor?"

"Everyone knows we are the children of Satan, but we did not spring fully formed from his forehead, like the goddess Athena from Zeus'."

"Do you know who it was?"

"There are rumors, of course. And the text, which I think makes it obvious. But there are those who deny it, and the prophecies."

"These are *prophecies*?" Her eyes narrowed. "Wait, can *you* read them?"

He shook his head. "No. No one here can. But someone has had some of them translated years ago."

She bit her lip.

Godric stared at the wall, his face expressionless. "It's ancient angelic."

How on earth was she able to do *that*?

"Why would the Mortus have ancient angelic on its walls..."

No.

That wasn't possible.

"You're saying you think the Mortus were born from the union between *an angel* and Satan?"

"Took you a while to piece that together," Godric muttered.

"But the Mortus are *evil*."

He tapped his fingers against his thigh. "So are some angels."

She wanted to argue that point, but she knew her mother thought the same. However, the only angel Peony had known was *good*, the kind of good she'd always wanted in her life. She couldn't picture Z having had a relationship with a demon, let alone with someone as notorious and destructive as Satan.

"I have photographed many of the walls," he said. "I will give you some of the images to study. Just don't tell anyone you're doing it."

"Why?"

"Because my uncle will want to kill you even more."

"Why hasn't he done it already?" Peony asked, curious despite herself.

"I have convinced him not to, for the moment."

"How kind of you." Each word dripped sarcasm.

His mouth quirked in a sardonic smile, then he turned and began walking back in the direction they had come.

"You said something about prophecies?" she asked, her mind still reeling.

"Oh yes, we have a great many. My favorite is how a demon from three worlds will come to the Mortus, dethrone the king, be crowned in front of angels and bring forth a new age."

She couldn't tell if he was being sarcastic or not. "You don't think that's possible?"

Just the angel part alone sounded crazy.

No angels would step foot in the Mortus den. She considered Z: he'd been as kind to her as he could be, given their differences and his position as a slave, but he had still hated demons. Even he would never come here.

Godric smiled, the expression filled with malice. "Well, it hasn't happened yet, and the Mortus have been around almost as long as Hell has existed. But who knows? Tomorrow could be our lucky day."

CHAPTER 29

They arrived back at the harem's communal area to find Lady Eramine in the path of the king, deliberately blocking him.

"Mother, *move*."

The duchess gave the monarch a glacial stare. "Did you forget your manners in the last day or so?" She oozed disdain.

Peony winced in sympathy. Only a parent could deliver that kind of withering comment without blinking.

The king drew his shoulders back. "I am the king. I gave you an order."

"And I am your mother. I gave you life. I can take it away just as easily."

Ouch.

"Uncle Alvin was never Grandmother's favorite," Godric whispered, almost like they were at a show and he was explaining an important plot point.

"Then who was?" she asked.

He gave her a sidelong glance. "Uncle Clement, but he's been missing for decades."

"I didn't think parents were meant to have favorites." At least, that's what she'd been told. Being an only child, she had always been Selene's favorite.

He gave a soft laugh. "That's hilarious."

Godric's chuckle drew the attention of the king and Lady Eramine. They froze for a brief instant, then turned matching glowers on him.

"What are you doing with *that*?" the king demanded.

I must be 'that'. I'm a person, damnit!

Funny how she didn't appreciate being reduced to nothing more than a thing. It's what Trick and the Infernus had done to Z, and she'd hated it then, too. She experienced a soft pang at the thought of the angel—she hoped Sylvester had kept his word and not hurt Z, and that Trick hadn't cut the angel's wings off to aid in his healing. Then again, none of that would matter when it came to Dru: for her, it would be simply about whether she thought the angel was a threat to the guild.

Peony decided not to contemplate that eventuality: Z was alive and all was well.

There. Positive thinking 101.

"We went for a walk," Godric said smoothly. "I was trying to determine if she had any idea as to her father's identity."

They hadn't spoken of her father at all, but she wasn't about to quibble with their alibi.

Lady Eramine opened her mouth to speak, but King Alvin got there first.

"It is of no consequence who she is related to," he growled. "She is female and a cambion. Unless we can work out how to breed her, then she is of little value to us." He met Peony's stare. "You're on borrowed time as it is, girl."

Anger flared in the pit of her stomach. Women were worth more than their value as breeding stock.

She was worth more.

The king turned back to Lady Eramine. "Why haven't you sent the girl as I requested?"

"She is still not healed."

"That is irrelevant. She has a duty to perform."

Lady Eramine looked around the communal area—her frosty gaze so like Godric's that the familial relationship seemed obvious now—as if to determine that they were alone. "You damaged her badly, Alvin. A broken skull and spine, plus damage I could not heal. She had to be stitched back together by your abomination."

Alvin's chin went up. "She is the sister of traitors. It is an honor that I chose her as the receptacle of my seed. She could be the mother of the next Mortus king."

He is responsible?

The slow-burning anger that had been kindled within Peony grew hotter and hotter, until she could barely think straight. He'd tried to hit her seconds after meeting her—gods knew what he'd tried to do to Dru—and then he'd abused Milly mercilessly. Who knows what else he'd done over the years? Or what he would do in the future?

"You can pick someone else for tonight," the duchess said. "She needs time to heal. She still has sutures."

Peony could sense Godric's surprise at his grandmother's refusal of the king's demands.

"I want her." Alvin sounded petulant, like a child whose favorite toy had been confiscated due to bad behavior.

"You can't have her." Peony strode to stand in front of the king, dodging around Godric as he tried to restrain her. She crossed her arms over her chest and stood next to Lady Eramine, who reacted to Peony's statement with a slight curl to her lip.

"You *dare* to forbid me *anything*?" The king's face was caught between incredulousness and rage.

"I am a doctor. I will protect my patient."

"You're nothing more than a broodmare, and you can't even do that!"

He spat at her, the thick globule hitting her in the face. Nauseated, she wiped the body fluid away with her sleeve, her anger ramping up even further.

"If you touch that girl, I will kill you."

Instantly, she regretted her threat. *I am not a murderer! I will not break my promise!*

She would not become like Dru, like the king,

But her mother's voice rang out in her mind. '*If you watch a horror happen, and don't stop the perpetrator, you are just as bad as that horror.*' That's why Selene meted out her own brand of justice on the rapists and abusers she could identify from victims in the ER.

"You wouldn't even touch Lord Farcon," the king said. "Your threat means nothing."

Peony balled her hands into fists.

He was innocent.

Well, innocent of any crimes Peony knew of. He was probably just as horrible as the king, though, if all male Mortus demons were like him.

The king turned on his mother. "Now, get me the girl."

"No."

Alvin backhanded Lady Eramine in the face, the blow so quick Peony didn't have time to intervene. Shock flared in the demon's eyes and she dabbed at her lip, which had begun to bleed. Her expression gave no evidence of the pain she must be suffering.

"Uncle—" Godric stepped forward, his hand outstretched toward his grandmother.

Alvin didn't look at his nephew, his anger still focused on his parent. "Bring me the girl, Godric, or that will just be the first round of punishment meted out to your grandmother."

Lady Eramine's head tilted back. "You would dare to 'punish' me? After all I have done for you?"

"Done for me? You have done *nothing* for me, just for the good of the race."

Godric quickly disappeared from view.

He isn't going to get Milly, is he?

"I have kept these women alive for the past three decades!" Lady Eramine snapped. "If left to your 'use', they would have died."

"Nonsense. We are immortal."

"We can still bleed out. Or die from severe wounds. Many of these women are still young and not fully settled into their immortality."

Another crack sounded, and a welt appeared on Lady Eramine's other cheek. She smiled, her teeth covered in blood, her gray eyes glistening ominously. "Is that all you can do?"

This family is crazy.

Lady Eramine was basically asking for more pain. More violence.

Godric reappeared then, Milly following a few

hesitant steps behind. Fear pinched her features, especially when she spotted Peony standing near the king.

How could Godric have retrieved her? Yes, Peony had known that he was Mortus; but he hadn't seemed like the kind of guy who would enable a rapist. He had seemed more complex; like the blonde female she'd met. That compassion and laughter could exist in a place like this. Godric was interested in ancient texts, in taking her around for a walk. In listening to her—at least a little bit, which was more than the king had done.

Shows what I know.

Then Peony registered Milly glancing between the king and *her*.

Does she think I'm his executioner?

Peony's skin crawled at the idea.

"Your Majesty." Milly wobbled a curtsey, wincing with pain from the movement.

He wants to take her to bed even now.

The king's eyes glittered; as if the injured woman was even more appealing now than she had been when healthy.

"Come with me," the king demanded.

Milly's eyes filled with tears, but she took a tentative step forward. Alvin grinned with relish.

Peony stepped between the female Mortus and the king. "No."

Even though she was half-expecting it, the blow to her stomach made her muscles seize, and the air flee her lungs. Gasping, she clutched both hands to her abdomen as the king lashed out again, slamming the blade of his foot into her knee. Crying out, Peony dropped to the floor.

Breathe, just breathe.

Fighting for air, she raged at her helplessness.

You're wearing gloves, you could have hit him.

But she wasn't a warrior like Dru—she only knew basic self-defense.

The king looked down at her on the floor, shaking his head. "Pathetic." He stepped over her, toward Milly.

Lady Eramine moved forward again, but this time Alvin lashed out with a blade. The knife sank deep into his mother's thigh, and she grunted at the impact, but remained standing. Blood seeped from the wound through the dove-gray of her skirts.

Alvin leaned toward her. "Get in my way again, and it goes in your heart."

Shock flashed briefly across Lady Eramine's face before it smoothed to its previous calm. "You are a disappointment."

"That's nothing new," Alvin snapped in return. He reached a hand out to Milly, who stared at it as if it were a cobra poised to attack. "Come here, *now.* Or your head will join your brother's in the display chamber."

Display chamber?

Get up. Get up, stop being useless.

Dru wouldn't stand for this.

Then again, half the Mortus den would be dead by now if Dru had a say in it.

Peony tried to shove herself to her feet, but her knee protested, and she collapsed back to the ground. Lying there, weak and useless, her cheek pressed against the floor, she stared at the king's legs. His shoes were black and polished to such a high shine, she could see her face reflected in them—wide eyes looking helplessly back at herself.

Disgust welled up deep within her.

Get up!

As she propped her hands underneath herself to try and rise, she noticed a tiny patch of bare skin where the king's pants leg ended and his shoe began. She mentally measured the distance between herself and the king.

It was impossible. He'd crush her before she reached him.

Try anyway.

You must not break your promise!

Milly placed her hand in the king's, drawing Peony's attention away from her internal conflict. Tears marked the girl's cheeks, still mottled with bruises that had yet to completely fade.

"I bestow on you an honor; stop wasting your tears," the king said, smarmy now he had his way.

He will kill her this time, and anyone who stands in his way.

Peony ripped off her glove and stretched her arm out.

"Uncle?" Godric called.

The king turned slowly toward his nephew.

Just do it.

Lunging, she grabbed the king's leg, her hand scrabbling under his trousers.

"What are you—?" He kicked at her, but she rolled to the side.

Grabbing on with a strength she didn't know she had, she slid her hand around until bare skin met her exposed fingers.

"You fucking whore!" He lashed out with his free foot, connecting with her ribs. She heard the crack before the pain hit her, sharp and penetrating.

Fractured rib.

Gritting her teeth through the agony, she dug her nails into his calf, until blood ran.

Why isn't he dying?

She met Godric's stare, calculating and intense.

A low, agonized groan filled the room, fine tremors streaking through the king's body. Peony let go and scrambled away, bile bitter in the back of her throat.

What have I done?

Seconds later, the king collapsed on the ground, seizing. Bloody foam frothed at his mouth, and his jaw worked, although no sound emerged.

Then he was still.

You have betrayed yourself.

He had to be stopped. And with demons, there was only one way to be certain they wouldn't come back after you...

"You killed him," Lady Eramine whispered, staring at the lifeless body of her son. She jabbed a finger at Godric. "And you helped."

"Me? I was standing over here, I did nothing." Godric held both hands up, palms out, as if curiously amused by his uncle's demise.

I don't understand these people...

The older Mortus spun on Peony. "You cursed abomination—"

"Come now, is that any way to talk to your long-lost granddaughter?" Godric asked, stepping over to Peony and offering her a gloved hand.

Peony stared at it for a few moments, before taking it and allowing him to help her up. She hobbled over to a seat and collapsed, wiping sweat and blood from her face. Shock at her actions still surged through her. *I am a murderer now. My word means nothing.*

Wait.

"Did you say granddaughter?" Peony asked, mind catching on that statement, despite her ribs screaming at her.

"I am fairly sure you are Uncle Clement's daughter," Godric replied.

"Her lineage is irrelevant," Lady Eramine said.

"Fairly sure?" Peony said, ignoring her. "On what evidence?"

She had no idea who her father was, so how could Godric know?

"The fact you have gray eyes and look like Clement," Lady Eramine snapped.

"You suspected?" Godric shot his grandmother a surprised look.

"I have eyes in my head, and Clement was *my* son. I also know he had found his fated mate before he disappeared."

"Disappeared? As in ran away or died?" Peony asked. The hope that her father might still be alive was a new, painful sensation.

"Murdered, mostly likely by Alvin. He never could tolerate competition, and your father had been named heir by my husband."

How fast her emotions crashed.

"So, wait." She held a hand up, her head throbbing in time with her knee and ribs. "My father was meant to be the king of the Mortus?"

"You got it, princess," Godric said.

"Princess?" She gulped.

"Well, queen now, I guess." He shrugged, as if the statement was neither here nor there.

"*Queen*?"

A slow, satisfied smile crossed Godric's face. "Your father was the rightful king. Therefore, you and your sister are ahead of me in the line of succession."

"There cannot be a queen, we only have kings," Milly said in a quiet voice.

"You forget the prophecy. 'One day a daughter of the Mortus and Nephilim will rule; born of three worlds, she will be crowned in the presence of angels, and her touch will be deadly to all.' I think she fits most of the criteria."

"Except you don't see an angel around here," Peony protested. "And my mother was human."

Her birth-mother, anyway.

Selene, on the other hand... Her mother's lineage was a secret that Peony had been forbidden to even *think* about.

"I am happy to overlook that little detail," Godric said.

"You—" Lady Eramine growled.

"What? Don't tell me you were happy with Alvin's rule. And since daddy-dearest has also been MIA for thirty years, it's not like he's going to come back and take over the Mortus. Or do you want the job, Grandmother?"

"Don't get cheeky with me, boy."

"No, ma'am."

"I've been waiting for *you* to take the crown," Lady Eramine grumbled. "Whose side are you on, anyway?"

Godric's smirk disappeared. "Mine. Always mine." Then he checked his watch and gave a low laugh.

"Guess what?" he said, looking over at Peony. "It's after midnight."

CHAPTER 30

One moment, Z was standing in the mansion, the next, he was in a hallway that led off a cavernous stone-walled entryway. Dark basalt soared overhead, and the scent of sulfur and woodsmoke was rich and potent. His skin tingled with the bite of magic, and the taste of evil lingered on his tongue.

They were back in Hell.

Osiris clapped his hands and the surrounding smoke dissipated. He'd teleported them here without the use of a Devilsgate, which meant the deposed god was powerful. More powerful than he should be, considering his magical abilities should have been stripped during the Great Culling.

So Azrael and Yael fought his brother, Set. And Yael cut off Set's head, but Set supposedly still lives...

Did the archangels know of this?

That kind of immortality went against their teachings...

Z scanned the hall—empty except for their small team of himself, Azrael and Osiris—and took note of the exits.

He was careful to keep his healed wings tucked tight to his body. He didn't want to give the enemy an easy target. Next to him, Azrael bared his teeth in what might have passed for a smile, if you ignored the unholy light in his eyes.

"You have no idea how much I want to kill some of the assholes here," he muttered, when he caught Z staring.

Z couldn't recall a single time when they'd worked together in Heaven that Azrael had cursed. In fact, Z had wanted to be like Azrael in another four hundred years. Not so anymore. *We've all changed...*

"Yael is going to be so mad we left him at home," Azrael added.

Z wasn't sure what he was meant to say to that. "Oh?"

"Yeah, he's still dark about me and Dru. The fact that we get to go on a killing spree without him? Jealousy to the max."

"Okay." Z had already worked out that Yael would like nothing more than to slit Dru's throat, but his loyalty to Azrael prevented it—barely. It seemed to Z that Yael was simply waiting for a good enough excuse; kill first, ask for forgiveness later.

To be fair, Z wasn't sure how successful Yael would be. Dru was an assassin, and a good one, from the sound of it. Plus, Z knew firsthand how strong Peony was, and she was a healer; she hadn't spent years training to become the perfect weapon, like Dru.

A few seconds later, Dru appeared from nowhere, holding hands with the male cambion who had healed Z back in the guild, and an imp whose dark eyes glimmered maniacally. It reminded him of Trick and the throbbing handprint on his torso.

The sight of the cambion healer sent a ripple of dislike through him—why had Dru involved the guild?

That hadn't been part of the plan. All she had said was that she was going to grab a few extra weapons before meeting them here.

Dru let go of the two newcomers and turned to them, her expression alert. The males studied the area around them within seconds, before focusing on Azrael, Z and Osiris.

"Az," Dru said, "this is Sylvester and Metcalf. Guys, this is Az, my man. Fuck with him and prepare to be knifed."

The two demons nodded, like the threat was par for the course.

She waved a hand in his direction. "And this is Z."

"Dude is an angel," the imp said, running his tongue over his lips.

Dru frowned. "Bite him and you'll piss off Peony."

"Why would that annoy Doc?"

"She spent weeks healing him," Sylvester replied, running a hand over his hair.

"Pity. I always wanted to taste angel."

"Another time," Sylvester said, voice consoling.

I don't think so.

"Who's the other guy?" Metcalf asked.

"No one you need to remember," Osiris said, his voice hypnotic.

Z wondered if the god had just laid a spell on the two demons.

Sylvester clapped his hands together and focused on Dru. "So, what's the deal here? How do we rescue Doc?"

Something like anger settled in Z's gut—he didn't like that this demon had a nickname for Peony. She was *his* healer. Nor did he like the fact that the other demon was a cambion and passably attractive.

Peony didn't need them—Z would save her.

"If the rumors of the Mortus den are true, you'll most likely find her in a harem," Osiris said.

"*A* harem?" Z asked. "There is more than one?"

The idea of Peony being used by anyone made a red haze descend over his vision. He'd kill anyone who touched her.

"From what I've heard, there are a few. One for the soldiers, one for the commoners, and one for the nobles."

"Sounds like too much hard work," Metcalf said. "They should just do what we imps do—let the woman chose and be ready for when they're in season." He guffawed.

"I've seen your men; the woman would have a tough time choosing which one to pick," Dru muttered.

Z wasn't sure if that was a compliment or an insult.

"When did you see other Reynard's Imps?" Metcalf demanded.

"Let's go rescue Doc, then worry about Dru's murdering of your kind later," Sylvester said.

Z agreed.

"Shall we find a few guards, hurt them, and find out where Peony is?" Azrael asked.

"That was the original plan," Dru said drily.

"The original plan was to subdue anyone we saw here, but the hallways are empty," Z said, studying the main tunnel.

"Where to next?" Sylvester asked.

Osiris nodded, as if coming to a decision. "I can't be here any longer. My brother will detect me soon, and another war with Set is something I am not prepared to undergo just yet. Say my name three times when holding this and I will come to extract you." The god handed Z a pebble, the edges smoothed over time by the flow of water.

It looked like a regular rock, but his skin prickled where it contacted the stone. "Thank you."

Eyes the color of sunrise examined Z's face, as if searching for an answer to an unasked question. "If you save Selene's daughter, that will be thanks enough."

Then the god vanished in a cloud of black smoke.

"Uh, you didn't say there'd be any deposed gods involved in this," Melcalf said to Dru.

"There aren't. He's gone now."

"Hmph. Gods make everything worse."

"Yes, I know that," Dru said. Then she turned to Azrael. "So, is Set still really alive?"

The Dart ran a hand over her arm affectionately. "We can worry about that later."

She nodded.

Z was on edge; the longer they delayed here, arguing over trivia, the more danger Peony was in. "Let's go."

They slinked silently down the hallways, Azrael and Dru on point, while Sylvester and Metcalf guarded their backs. Z wasn't too happy having two demons behind him, but he was the weakest one among them, so his position in the center made sense, even if it hurt his pride.

In a small room with a delicate fireplace and vintage setting they finally encountered a guard. Cloaked, he stood at attention near an internal door, but dropped into a fighting stance when he spotted them.

"Where's my sister?" Dru growled, prowling toward him.

He didn't answer. Instead, he launched an attack, shouting as he did so. Before he even landed a strike, Dru had him on the ground, razor-sharp claws at his throat. Her actions were so fast, Z had trouble tracking them.

"Last time I was here, we established that I can kill your kind with these," Dru said, flexing her claws. "So, I'll ask again, where is my sister?"

"Sis-sister?"

"She looks like me. Hard to miss."

"I don't know anyone like that." The guard wet his lips, eyes flicking toward the door he'd been guarding.

Z's internal lie-detector screamed: the guard knew Peony.

But Dru didn't need telling.

"I don't like liars." She slashed his throat. Blood sprayed in an arterial arc, and she stepped back with a sigh. She wiped her face with her sleeve, leaving smears of crimson behind.

Z stared.

This cold-eyed woman was *nothing* like his healer, despite sharing the same face.

"Death is always so messy."

"The way you do it, sure," Sylvester said. "But you don't need to go around slashing throats to get the job done."

"What?" Dru looked defensive. "If I'd used my toxin, it would have been just as messy."

"I'll have to teach you a trick or two."

"You're more of a thief than an assassin anyway. You

prefer to pilfer."

"I am a man of many talents."

Ignoring them, Z strode toward the door. It was locked, but he would be able to break through the wooden panel easily. Stepping back to allow himself room, he paused when a hand came down on his shoulder.

"I got this." Sylvester stepped by him and dropped to one knee. Within seconds, there was a click. "It was barely worth the effort."

"Back in formation," Azrael ordered, then took the lead. He opened the door, and they immediately heard shouts and screams beyond. The Dart used a small tube-like device to peer around the corner.

"There's a mob there, centered on something. Maybe we should go a different way?" He held up the device again and cursed. "Never mind. It's centered on your sister."

Peony.

Z's mind went blank, and suddenly he was through the door, his gloved hands striking out at the rioting Mortus demons. *Don't touch their skin.* The litany helped calm him, but it took months, years, to finally locate the white-blonde hair of his healer.

There.

His blood surging through his veins, he slammed through the mob, leaving unconscious bodies in his wake. The weakness that had plagued him for months was gone, strength pulsing within him at the sight of his healer.

Peony was shaking, clumsily fighting off the Mortus who approached her.

Next to her, a tall male Mortus battled with lethal intent, felling demon after demon, all the while wearing an icy, detached smile. An older female demon on Peony's other side struck out with a knife, most of her attackers seeming afraid to approach her.

A fist slammed into Z's side, cracking a rib. Without pausing, he slammed the hilt of his knife into his assailant's face, hearing the satisfying crunch of a broken nose.

Then he was in front of Peony.

He ripped away the Mortus who was attacking her, throwing him halfway across the room, then took position in front of her. No one was getting through him.

"Z?" Peony's eyes were wide with shock. "What are you doing here? Your wings!"

A Mortus approached, wielding a sword, but Dru stepped smoothly in the way and sliced her claws across his arm. He dropped to the floor, screaming in agony.

Shouts rang through the crowd now, and weapons were slowly lowered. Dead bodies littered the carpet and tiles, blood and viscera smeared over every surface. Vacant eyes stared upward.

The team formed a loose circle around Peony and the two Mortus demons who'd fought alongside her. A bruised female was crouching on the floor between them, her hands over her head.

Z's eyes raked over Peony, looking for injuries. She seemed well, although she was hunched slightly. He was happy to just see her.

It's relief.

The male demon, meanwhile, was gazing flatly at Dru. "You're back."

Dru grimaced. "Just to get my sister."

"That might be a problem."

"Why?" Azrael demanded.

The demon crossed his arms over his chest. "Because she's our new queen."

Their *what*?

CHAPTER 31

Chaos.

Peony's world had descended into chaos.

One minute they had been moving the dead body of the king, the next, a mob had descended on the harem's communal area. She had fought for her life, but even then she'd kept her ungloved hand away from any bare Mortus skin.

She already felt dirty, sick.

The king had deserved to die, but she shouldn't have been the one to mete out justice. No matter what her mother believed, Peony didn't have the right to decide who lived and died. She had broken a vow she'd made to herself the day her skin had turned toxic.

She had killed.

Then, almost as quickly as the melee had begun, it was over, thanks to arrival of several newcomers. And her world, already skewed, had tilted.

Peony stared in shock at Z.

He was so...*healthy*.

Her fingers itched to stroke his magnificent wings, to

feel those white feathers that looked soft as silk. He was still thin—his jawline was sharp enough to cut glass—but his green eyes blazed.

He was so handsome it hurt.

Belatedly, she focused on the others: Dru, a dark-haired man she didn't know, Sylvester, and Metcalf. What were they doing with Z? How had Metcalf learned of the angel? Had Trick sent them to come and get her?

That thought died a quick death.

Trick wouldn't renege on a deal. Her former boss was focused on profit and reputation. Saving her would never have entered his mind.

"She's your *queen*?" Dru demanded.

Peony flinched.

Godric raised an eyebrow. "I was speaking clearly, wasn't I?"

"Enough of this nonsense!" Lady Eramine snapped. She drew up to her full height and stared at the assembled Mortus. They had *not* accepted Godric's claim that Peony was now their ruler.

Neither had Peony, for that matter.

Lady Eramine projected her voice across the room. "You have a new ruler. This abom—I mean, demon—killed the king. Through her right, she is now queen."

One of the males in the crowd shouted, "We will not be ruled by a woman!"

A number of shouts echoed his sentiment.

"But you can be killed by one," Dru called back, flashing her claws. That silenced the dissenters quickly.

"The coronation will take place now." Lady Eramine shot a meaningful look at Godric.

Now?

Why not tomorrow? That way Peony could try to convince them that this was ridiculous. She could at least arrange for a DNA test to be done, so that she could prove she wasn't related to Lady Eramine and Godric, and was therefore ineligible for the throne.

I do not want to be queen. I want to leave.

"But I may not be related to you—" Peony began.

Lady Eramine glared. "It's too late now."

Godric disappeared behind the sofa, to where the king's body had been dragged before the demons rioted. He returned quickly, something silvery glinting in his hand. He handed the crown to Lady Eramine, who took hold of it by her fingertips, like it was diseased.

Peony took a step back, but a hand clamped down on her upper arm. She turned to Lady Eramine, who murmured, "You made your bed, lie in it. You want our women to be treated better? Ensure it."

She bit the inside of her cheek. Had she known this would await her, she would have tried something slightly less fatal to resist the king.

"I don't want to be queen," she said quietly.

"Yes, but I don't want to be king, so suck it up," Godric murmured, close to her ear. Then, without warning, he shouted, "All hail the new queen!"

Lady Eramine shoved the crown on her head.

Peony's back bowed as magic slammed through her. A scream built in her throat as tears swam at the back of her eyes, but she remained silent, her entire body locked in an agony so intense, black spots danced in her vision.

The rock beneath her feet grew warm, until she couldn't sense where she ended, and the den began. With every rapid beat of her heart, power settled through her body, linking her to all the Mortus there present, and beyond, their life sparks scattered throughout Inferno.

Inferno, its lifeblood and power, had become part of her soul. And with it, she was attuned to every Mortus in existence—an oily presence under her skin that spoke of an inborn malevolence she knew she instinctively she lacked.

Then it was over.

Panting, Peony opened her eyes. Her sight, which had already been good, was now exceptional. She could see the finest details on the cloth worn by members of the harem, who stood poised on the edges of the room, as if ready for flight. She drew her attention back to her friends, to Z.

A faint glow surrounded him now, a silver aura she'd never been able to see before. It made her blood pump faster, but not from discomfort this time. She quickly shoved the emotional response aside and scanned the others. Dru glowed a black-threaded-silver, while Sylvester was outlined in gray. Metcalf was pure black, and the stranger was silver like Z, although his aura had faint whisperings of ebony. He must be an angel, too, although he didn't have wings.

She looked at her hands and saw a burning green glow, finely threaded with darkness. By comparison, the Mortus in the room were cloaked with black-threaded-green.

Black must be for demons.

Silver is for angels...

What does green mean?

She'd have to ask someone, but not now. Feeling the expectant stares on her, she drew herself up straight. "Go back to your rooms. Everyone. I will decide what to do about you and your disrespect tomorrow."

Peony didn't know where the bravado came from, but the Mortus must have seen something in her expression, because they cleared out of the room, quickly.

Then it was just her, Dru and the others, Lady Eramine, Godric and Milly.

"Milly, go back to the infirmary," Lady Eramine snapped.

The injured demon slunk out of the room.

Then the duchess bristled at Dru. "*You.*"

Peony's twin flashed a mocking smile. "Me!"

"*You're* the reason all of this has happened."

"I'd say it's the king's fault," Dru snapped. "But I gather he's dead."

"Very," Godric murmured drily.

"You need to come back with us," Dru said, turning hard eyes on her

She looks like Lady Eramine.

It was then Peony realized a DNA test would be useless. The evidence of their relationship was there in front of her; Dru and Lady Eramine may not share a face, but their expressions and their eyes were the same.

Funny how she's my twin, but she seems more like a full-blooded Mortus than me.

Plus, Peony now wore a crown that bound her to Hell. She didn't think anything other than death would sever the connection.

Can I even leave here? Ever?

"She can't go with you," Godric said. "Aside from the fact she's a blood-bound slave, she's also our new queen."

Trapped.

Panic seized her, until a field of emerald green came into view.

Z.

He placed his hands on her shoulders, and a deep sense of calm enveloped her.

Then she realized he was touching her.

A quick glance confirmed he was wearing gloves—he was safe—but she stepped back anyway, breaking the contact.

The warmth lingered.

I could become addicted to that. To the sense of belonging he evoked, even for a few seconds; to the feeling that everything was right in the world when, clearly, everything *wasn't*.

Peripherally, she saw Metcalf creep closer to Dru. "Hey, Dru, your ring is glowing—"

Peony frowned. Dru had never worn jewelry before.

"It's so shiny," Metcalf said as he reached out to the stone.

Dru tried to snap her hand away, panic on her face, "No, don't touch—"

Dru and the imp vanished.

The dark-haired stranger lunged toward the duo, cursed as he stumbled against thin air. "Fuck!"

Z spun back. "Azrael!"

"That damned imp just teleported them."

"Where?" Peony demanded.

"To Metcalf's chosen destination," the stranger—Azrael?—said. "I am going to have to cut that damned ring off her finger."

"That leaves the three of us, and a whole heap of dead Mortus," Sylvester said, sounding bored. But something wicked glinted in his expression. "And considering I am doing this pro bono, I have to get back to my lovely master ASAP."

He looked at her, serious. "Doc, are you really stuck here?"

Miserably, Peony nodded. Would she ever be able to see her mother again? Selene couldn't travel to Hell, not for longer than a few minutes, at any rate.

"Then I'll come visit," Sylvester said. "Kisses!" He strode out of the room, carefully stepping around the bodies like they were furniture.

Kisses?

"Where are you going?" Azrael called.

"I've got my own way home," Sylvester called over his shoulder. "You need anything, Doc, you know where to find me. Catchya!"

She saw the look on Z's face—his beautiful green irises were hard as jade, and his jaw was clenched. "Are you with...him?" The angel's voice was low and intense.

Peony gave an awkward shrug. "No, that's just Sylvester. He likes to joke around."

But something warm expanded in her belly—was Z jealous?

That's ridiculous.

No, that's hopeful thinking.

CHAPTER 32

The idea of Peony with that...*male* made Z's blood heat and his pulse race.

But why did it matter?

He's nothing more than a demon who will take advantage of her.

Yes, that was it.

When had his desire to bring her home—to simply return the favor of her assistance—changed to actually caring for her?

You don't know her.

He knew she was strong, kind, and inherently *good*. The fact she was the new Mortus queen was worrying, but might was right in the three circles of Hell. It meant that she had killed the former king; not that she was actually like the Mortus in any way. He just hoped that the former monarch hadn't hurt her before she'd been forced to slay him.

He would have deserved it.

Azrael sighed. "I will wait here until Dru and that idiot imp return."

"You aren't welcome," the male Mortus snapped, his eyes crystalline.

"He stays," Z growled.

No Mortus would dictate to them. And considering their former role in the Heavens, Z and Azrael should be killing this demon on sight.

The demon gave Z a scathing glare, eyes raking over his wings. "*Your* kind is definitely not welcome."

Z spread them out, defiant. The stench of blood and death was thick in the room, but he ignored it.

Peony sighed. "They can come with me."

"And where are you going?" the elder Mortus woman demanded.

"The infirmary, to check on Milly."

"Leave that to me." The demon spun on her heel, her posture ramrod straight. "The angels may stay for now."

Peony drew herself up to her full height. "The angels may stay because I said they could. Is that clear?"

The females took the measure of each other for a few seconds before the older woman nodded, something like grudging respect on her face.

"I am going to leave you for now," said the male Mortus. "I need to go and wash the blood off. But you— angel-boy—" he pointed at Azrael, "—we are going to have a chat when I return."

When he'd gone, Z turned to Azrael. "Do you mind giving us some privacy?"

The Dart stared at him for a few moments, then nodded, a smile flashing across his face. "Sure. I might go and retrace our steps, in case Dru has returned."

Azrael slid a strap off his shoulder and slung his backpack to his front. He withdrew an item wrapped in cloth, returned the pack to its original position and handed the object to Z, who took it without thinking. It was spherical and freezing cold to the touch—the iciness burned his hand even through the wrapping and his glove.

"Give this to her," Azrael murmured. "Get her to look at it as soon as you can."

"The Orb?"

The Dart nodded.

Z's hand clenched around the magical object, and he ignored the icy pain in his palm. What was this minor discomfort after everything he had been through in the past few months?

Azrael silently left the hall, leaving Z to study the carnage. "This will need tidying up."

Peony bit her lip, her expression turning sad. "Such a waste of life."

"But they are Mortus." Z frowned.

"They were born demons, they can't help it." Peony almost sounded...defensive?

Then again, she was now queen of the race, at least until they worked out how she could abdicate. It only spoke of her warm nature that she should give these demons the benefit of the doubt.

"What happened?" Z asked, changing the topic. He doubted he'd ever be able to agree with her about the Mortus. After all, they weren't her kind, despite her crown.

"I could ask you the same thing." Her eyes roved over his wings. "You look much better than the last time I saw you."

Heat flooded his cheeks.

"Oh! I didn't mean that in a bad way...I'm happy you're healed." Now Peony's golden skin looked flushed, like she was embarrassed.

That makes two of us.

"Here, your sister and Azrael say you need this." Z thrust the Orb at her.

Peony stared at the object in his hand. "What is it? Why do I need it?"

"It's called Odin's Orb. It's a magical object that can allow you to see anything you want." At least, that was his understanding of it. It was demon magic—well, deposed-god magic—and that had never really been part of his lessons in Heaven. "Dru and Azrael—and me—need you to search for something."

"Why me?" She reached out a tentative hand, hovering it over the Orb.

"It can only be wielded by a demon who is 'pure of heart'."

She laughed. "I'm certainly not 'pure'."

Truth. So far as she saw it

How could she not realize how unique she was?

"Trust me, Dru and I think you are the perfect—the only—person to use this object."

"I think you may both have concussion."

She didn't believe him.

Could he have been wrong?

No. He knew her, knew bone-deep that her soul was pure, no matter that she had killed. Even the meekest animal would turn vicious when protecting its own. And Peony viewed her patients as hers. He'd seen the bruises on the girl they had sent back to the infirmary. She would have done anything to protect her.

He ran his free hand over his hair. "Take it."

Peony inhaled deeply then closed the distance between them, gently retrieving the Orb. She gasped at the contact.

Z jerked toward her, worried, but she stepped back, her eyes glued to the artifact.

"Are you all right?"

"It feels alive." Her voice was full of wonder.

"Alive?" The thing had nearly given him frostbite.

"Yes, it's warm."

That has to be a good sign.

"Why," she asked, "what did it feel like to you?"

"Freezing cold."

Peony unwrapped the cloth covering. "Odd."

Very. But then, demon magic didn't play well with angelic beings.

Exposed, the Orb glowed from within, fiery yellows and reds swirling chaotically together. It was mesmerizing.

"What am I meant to be looking for?"

"Heaven's Heart."

"Sorry, what?" Peony lowered her hands.

"It's a piece of a mystical artifact that had been kept safe in Heaven. It is what I was guarding when I was abducted by the Infernus. The others were punished because it was stolen."

"It was stolen? What does it look like?"

"I don't know."

Disbelief laced her words. "You don't know what it looks like?"

"It was so sacred no one but the archangels were allowed access to it."

"You said only part of it was kept in Heaven."

"There are two other pieces, but we don't know where they are, either."

"How am I meant to search for it, then?"

It was an excellent question. The others hadn't bothered to explain that.

"Maybe just think of a mystical object called Heaven's Heart. Think that you are looking for the stolen piece."

She bit her lip. "I don't know how effective that will be."

"Can you try?"

She sighed. "Of course I can *try*."

She focused her attention on the Orb. The colors changed, turning into a jade-green flame mixed with flickers of black.

"What do you see?" he asked, eager.

She stumbled, her cheeks flushing darker than before. "Can you see anything in the Orb? When I'm looking at it?"

"Just colors—green and black. Why?"

"Just curious."

Truth.

But he had a feeling it wasn't the whole truth.

She returned her focus to the Orb. He waited, breath held, until she shook her head. "I'm sorry, but I don't see anything."

Lie.

"Z? What's wrong?"

"He could tell you were lying," a voice said. The male Mortus had returned, clothing and skin free from gore. He held several sheets of paper in his hand.

"Lying?" Her voice held a slight tremor as she shoved

the Orb out of the demon's sight.

"Angels can tell when someone is lying, am I right?" The male strode closer, careful to avoid the corpses on the floor.

Z ground his teeth. "Yes."

"How could *you* tell I lied?" Peony asked the demon.

"I have a master's in body language."

Lie.

"You do?" Peony asked, eyes going wide.

The demon stared. "No, I was being sarcastic."

Truth.

"We need to do something about these bodies," the demon said.

Peony's demeanor changed subtly, from gentle to firm. "I can handle it, I think. But first, I want you to take an inventory of all the dead."

The demon tipped an imaginary hat at her. "You're the boss."

"Queen, actually."

"Here." The Mortus handed her the papers he was holding. Z peered at them—he'd been wrong, they weren't papers. They were photographs of some kind of writing. "These are the start of the script, I think."

Then the demon drew a notepad from his pocket, and strolled away, scribbling notes about the dead bodies as he went.

"Thanks, Godric!"

Z frowned at the photographs. "That is ancient angelic."

Peony nodded. "I know. Can you read it?" She held out the images.

He shook his head. "I know someone who could,

though."

Raze could no doubt understand the language.

"That's okay, I'll do it." Her voice was distracted as she scanned the pictures.

She'd translate? Since when had Peony learned ancient angelic?

"Here." Godric had returned, his inventory complete already.

"That's all of them?" she asked.

"Yes."

She narrowed her eyes. "That was awfully quick."

"I'm a fast worker."

"Hmmm."

"So, want me to bring in the soldiers to remove the corpses? Should I have them taken outside and burned?"

"What is the typical funerary tradition?" Peony asked.

Z didn't see the point in the question. They were the dead of the enemy—their bodies should be disposed of as quickly as possible.

"Cremation."

"Okay."

The fine hairs on the back of Z's neck and arms rose, and his skin tingled. He focused on Peony, to see her eyes had turned a shiny black, lit with green flames. His instinct was to withdraw from the power burning within her, but he forced himself to stand his ground. He noticed Godric *had* recoiled from her.

Peony clicked her fingers and he was overpowered by the stench of scorched flesh, but it was gone almost as soon as it began. Now, where the bodies had once lain, there were piles of ash scattered around the room.

"It's done," Peony said.

The green flame in her eyes had died, and as he watched, the black slowly bled away, until her gray irises returned.

"How did you *do* that?" Godric breathed.

"It's the crown, or the coronation. It linked me to the Mortus. I can feel Hellfire, too, so thought I would try calling it."

Z wiped a hand over his face. He had never heard of such a thing, but she hadn't lied.

Peony gave Godric and Z a worried look. "Couldn't the king do that?"

"No, he couldn't."

"Wonderful."

"Then again, he wasn't a prophesied ruler."

Z's breath caught in his throat.

There's a prophecy?

CHAPTER 33

Peony and Z were in the king's former study. The room was huge, with bookcases lining three walls, a large stone desk in the center, and a few scattered leather chairs. She didn't want to think about the kind of leather—knowing the Mortus, it could very well be human in origin. Despite the room's lack of dust, it had a distinct air of neglect. The photos Godric had given her were scattered on the desk's shiny surface—she'd only managed to read the first few lines.

'The Mortus are my gift to the world. Born of Satan and myself, they are balance. Their evil exudes from their very skin, their strength will stand the test of time, but their souls, these have the potential to be pure, should they but earn it.'

A demon with a pure heart.

Any Mortus had the potential to wield the Orb, but none had ever tried to earn the right.

Still, nothing felt real.

One moment, she'd been a blood slave, the next, queen of the Mortus. She could suddenly read ancient angelic scripts and create fire from nothing. Even now, the heat from Hell slunk through her veins, waiting for a chance to be released again. What kind of monster had she become?

At least Z had healed. His wings were a sight to behold—their beautiful white plumage soft and luxurious, and framing his figure in a way that would be imposing if she wasn't so fascinated by them. How had he managed it?

She set the Orb down on top of the photos. She'd just checked it for the fourth time—and again it hadn't shown her the stupid artifact. How was she meant to search for something she couldn't even picture?

Instead of showing her Heaven's Heart, it had shown her *her* heart. At least, the thing she desired above all else.

It had shown her Z.

She'd been so grateful that he couldn't see the images the Orb produced. It would have been beyond embarrassing if he realized she had a crush on him. Or worse, if he thought she was in love with him. He was a fully fledged angel, and she was, well, a cambion. The lowest of the low in the demon echelon.

Now you are a queen.

Of one of the most evil races to walk the Hells. It wasn't a rise in status, at least, not for an angel.

What is Mom going to say about this?

Nothing good, that was for sure.

"They said Trick sold you," Z said quietly, breaking into her thoughts.

Hoping he hadn't caught her staring at him like a lovesick fool, she nodded.

His jaw muscles flexed. "Did they hurt you?"

"No."

She wasn't about to tell him about the assassination attempt. He would probably try to take revenge on the girls—and Peony wasn't angry at them. Not anymore. Being kept as a narcissist's plaything was bound to make anyone crazy.

"You're lying."

Peony sighed. Angels and their stupid truth-detectors. Why hadn't she known about them?

"I got cut, but it's fine. I heal fast."

"How did you get hurt? Did the king do it?"

"How it happened isn't important, and the king didn't do it. But he deserved to die." She stared into Z's emerald eyes, daring him to contradict her.

"I have no doubt that is the case." His voice, no longer hoarse from pain, was deep and mesmerizing.

Suddenly, the distance between them seemed to vanish and Z was right in front of her. He smelled of soap and woodsmoke. She ached to feel the softness of his wings, to touch his skin and know his warmth. But she couldn't do that—wouldn't risk his life, not after he'd just healed and had another chance.

Plus, there was no guarantee he'd *want* her to touch him, either.

His eyes blazed and he leaned in, as if to kiss her.

Step away.

But she couldn't.

Then his words registered: "We need to find a way to save you from the Mortus. You aren't meant to be in this role, no matter what the prophecy says. You aren't like them."

The crushing disappointment took Peony by surprise, and she shoved the emotion away. She was *worse* than the

Mortus: nothing more than a cambion nightmare. She was foolish for even entertaining the fantasy that he might want more to do with her. *Be* more to her.

"There is no way to escape the Mortus," she said eventually and dropped her gaze, the intensity of his beauty too much for her.

Warmth exploded through her a moment later; the featherlight touch of his mouth on hers so pure, so perfect she thought she imagined it.

No! He's going to die!

She shoved him away, but Z took hold of her shoulders, holding her in place as his lips touched hers again. Her mind was swamped with sensation: Z was *kissing* her. His mouth was smooth and firm, and he tasted of mint. Her whole body became electrified, her breasts tightening and her stomach dancing with butterflies. Her hands ached to touch him, to explore the firm planes of his body.

No!

She broke free, her breathing too fast, her mind in turmoil. "What have you done?" she wailed.

Z stared at her a moment, confusion on his face. "What do you mean?"

His eyes rolled back in his head and he shook, limbs trembling. Peony hurried forward and helped guide his body to the floor, careful to spread out his wings. "No, no, no."

His emerald gaze was dim as it turned on her, his body straining, fighting the shaking, trying to control it. "What...happening?"

Tears dripped onto her gloved hands as she held them uselessly in her lap. There was nothing she could do. Her toxin was too virulent for him to survive.

There is no cure.

Why hadn't she tried to find a cure?

A sob caught in her throat, but she forced out the words, "You're dying."

The trembling came to a sudden halt, his jaw clenched, the tendons standing out on his neck in sharp relief. A low groan filled the room, so full of pain that her vision blurred with tears. She groped out a hand blindly, laying her palm over his chest, feeling the struggling beat of his heart.

"I'm so sorry, I should have been paying attention, I should have stopped you..."

He was still.

A scream filled the room, raw and ugly.

Her scream.

The door burst open and Godric rushed in, knives in his hands, ready to face whoever had attacked her. He stopped abruptly as he took in the tableau, saw no threats in the room.

"Why'd you kill him?"

Peony collapsed on Z's chest, wrapping her arms around his body tightly, willing him back to life. Which was impossible. She was too deadly; a freak of nature that should have been drowned at birth.

A hand stroked her head, trying to calm her.

"Do you have a death wish?" she snapped at Godric.

But Godric was standing on the other side of the room. He couldn't have...

Z?

He lay there, his chest moving, his eyes alive and alert, *his* hand in her hair.

"*How*?" she whispered.

"You have *got* to be kidding me," Godric sighed.

"What?" Peony turned to look at her cousin.

"He's your *mate*." He spat the last word, as if it was diseased.

Surprise lanced through her, following by a rush of giddiness so intense she thought she might fly up and float around the room.

I have a mate!

"What's going on?" Z asked, and gently pushed her aside, so he could sit. His wings spread out behind him and she flinched as she took in his plumage. She *had* damaged him.

"What is it?" he asked, reaching out a hand to rest on her shoulder.

She automatically shied away from his touch, but stopped herself. There was no need. He had survived. "Your wings..."

He moved one around until it was in his line of vision, and then he stared, quiet.

The once pristine white of his feathers was laced with filaments of jade green, bordering on black in some places.

The color of her aura.

He looked at her, his face curiously blank. "I don't understand."

"You didn't realize..." Godric said with a low whistle.

Even she could see he was baiting Z, but her mouth was so dry she couldn't talk.

His voice low, Z asked, "Realize what?"

Rather than the relish she expected, Godric replied seriously, "Peony is a Mortus cambion. Her skin is more toxic even than ours. The only way you could have survived was if you were her mate."

His blank eyes settled on Peony, and she waited for the horror. For him to realize he'd kissed the monster that even other monsters shunned.

"So that's why you didn't want to be touched back in the cell." Z sounded...thoughtful?

She nodded, still not trusting her voice.

"I'll leave you both to it." Godric said, closing the door behind him with a decisive click.

"Some angels can survive a Mortus demon's touch," Peony said, although she didn't know why. She *wanted* Z to be hers. "At least, those are the rumors."

"Do you think that is the case here?"

Peony clenched her hands in her lap. She desperately wanted it to *not* be the case, so she tried to think rationally. "I don't know."

She couldn't explain why his wings had changed, if it was a standard angelic trait.

"Can we try something?" he asked.

She nodded, still staring at her lap. *Don't hope, don't lie. He may not be yours.*

It scared her, though, how much she wanted him to be hers. For her to be his.

For the majority of her life, from the time she had hit puberty, real touch had been forbidden to her. No boyfriends, no good friends. No one she could just cuddle for comfort, or embrace with love.

She'd been alone.

Until now, she hadn't realized how lonely she'd truly been.

Finding Dru had helped, but it hadn't been enough to

fill the yearning she'd buried deep within.

A gentle touch under her chin made her glance up, to focus on Z, on the sharp angles of his face. His mouth pressed against hers again, the touch careful, as if she were made of spun glass—or as if he was afraid of being poisoned again.

She drew back at the thought.

"Did you not like it?" Z asked, his voice rough.

"I don't want to hurt you."

"I think that ship has sailed."

She flinched.

"I didn't mean—"

"It's okay, I understand." She tried to stand, but her legs were wobbly and she found herself kneeling on the ground, wrung out.

"You didn't like kissing me?" Z asked.

She jerked. "No!"

His expression closed.

"I mean, I did like kissing you. But—"

"But what?"

"I don't know," she said helplessly.

I'm scared.

That's what she really wanted to say. Her life had changed too much too quickly.

"We don't have to try again, I just thought it might help—" Z made to stand, and she knew in that instant that she couldn't afford for him to walk away.

He might never come back.

Lurching forward, she awkwardly grabbed the sides of his face with her gloved hands and pressed her mouth against his. For a few horrifying seconds, he didn't do anything, and she worried that he didn't want her, that she was the worst kisser in all the realms...

Then he kissed her back.

He soothed her panic with a soft press of his lips, and a sweep of his tongue along the seam of her mouth. She opened for him, surprised and delighted by the feel of his tongue against hers. She allowed him to lead the kiss at first, needing to learn how, wanting to see what he thought she'd like. Soon though, she grew impatient, and wrapped her arms around his neck, pressing her body flush against his. It felt like her skin was too tight; she was fire and molten want, her body quickly igniting as he swept a hand down her spine to cup her butt, pulling her even closer, until she couldn't tell where she ended and he began.

She broke away briefly, to catch her breath.

Z tucked her head under his chin, and she felt precious, protected. For a tiny moment in her life, she was special.

Slowly, she disengaged.

He was staring at her. "Wow."

"What?" She raised a hand to her hair, self-conscious.

"That was amazing."

"Really?" She turned around, so he couldn't see her blush. "I've never done it before."

Hands settled on her shoulders once again and Z spun her back toward him. "I was your first?"

"I couldn't before—my touch—"

A smile spread over his face, masculine satisfaction stamped on every feature. "I'm honored."

Hesitantly, she asked, "Was I yours?"

His expression became shuttered, and a lump formed in her throat. It shouldn't matter that he had more experience. That would be a good thing if they became a couple; at least one of them would know what to do.

I didn't think angels did carnal things.

"I've only done it with one woman before," he said. "It was more of an experiment than anything."

"Did you love her?"

He ran a hand over his hair. "I thought I did at the time, but I realized a while ago that I was in love with the idea of her."

That shouldn't have made her happy, but it did. Did that make her a shallow person?

He smoothed some hair from her face, then pressed his forehead against hers. "Should we try the Orb again?"

Biting back a sigh, she nodded. She wanted to keep kissing him, but considering how quickly her emotions swung from highs to lows, she figured that the Orb, at least, was safe.

"Let's give it another go."

CHAPTER 34

They had been taken on a tour of the Mortus den—the palatial part, at any rate. To Z, it had seemed like a lot of hallways punctuated by side rooms of varying degrees of wealth and ostentation. Considering it was kept largely for the king, his family, the harem, and the retainers, it had seemed rather extravagant.

"How many Mortus live here?" he asked.

Godric, their tour guide, stopped to look at him. "Why? So you know how many angels to bring to wipe us out?"

It showed how far he'd fallen, Z thought, that the idea hadn't occurred to him.

It would put Peony at risk.

And he wasn't willing to do that.

"Just curious," Z replied. Staying silent would only play to Godric's accusation.

"Around six thousand, I think," Peony said.

Godric's eyebrows rose. "How did you know that?"

"I can feel their life forces."

When the demon just stared at her, Peony shuffled a

little. "Isn't that normal?"

"No."

"So, your uncle couldn't do that? Or the fire-thing?"

"No."

"Oh." Peony glanced at the ground.

Z wrapped a green-threaded wing around her briefly, and she gave him a small smile in return, one that had his heart beating so loudly he was surprised she didn't comment on it.

He wanted to kiss her again.

Who was he kidding? He wanted to do more than that.

She'd never been kissed before.

In a way, he wished he hadn't been with Dina, because Peony could have been his first, too.

That's a dangerous thought.

Then again, everything about Peony was dangerous to him.

Z's mind was still reeling from what Godric had announced earlier—angels didn't *have* fated mates. Angels could *be* someone's mate, he supposed, but Peony wasn't destined to be *his*, not unless he chose it to be so.

And did he want to make a choice that would exile him from Heaven, forever?

You're already an exile.

While Heaven's Heart remained lost, yes, he was. But if the Darts managed to retrieve all three pieces, it could be his ticket back home.

Do you really think that's possible?

Z knew the others had tried to make their situation look more appealing than it was, that they weren't angry they had been punished for his and Dina's failure. But even they hadn't been able to pretend that their mission was anything other than impossible.

It would be a win if they could simply find the piece of the Heart that the Infernus had stolen.

Besides, now his wings were...different, would he be allowed back into Heaven's army even if they did find the missing pieces?

Godric reached the end of another hallway and swung open a gilded door to reveal a bedroom. "This was the king's main sleeping area."

Peony stepped up to the threshold and looked inside, her posture stiff. Z came up behind her, taking in the ornate silks, the huge bed, and the intricately carved wooden furniture. One wall contained a rack of whips, chains and other devices that looked like they excelled in producing pain. On the walls were paintings of naked women, all wearing expressions of fear.

His lip curled in distaste.

Goosebumps spread over the skin of his forearms as power seared through the room. In little more than a heartbeat, the bed, the 'toys' and all the paintings had been burned to ash.

Peony spun back toward him, her eyes a black field against which danced green flames; then she blinked, and they were clear again. "Go through the items that remain and keep anything you feel is of value," she said. "The next time I come back, anything left will join the piles of ash."

Godric nodded, although Z was pleased to note a tiny droplet of sweat dripped from the demon's brow to trickle down his cheek.

"Now, is everything ready for the conference?" Peony asked.

"Yes." He checked his watch. "It should start in around fifteen minutes."

"Excellent. Take us there."

Z followed again as Godric led them out of the king's chambers, and toward a short hall. The door opened back onto the communal room where Z had first seen Peony. The ashes that marked the dead were still present, but now a throne had been set up at the end of the room. Peony walked toward it, her steps determined, although her expression spoke to him of sadness.

"What's going on?" Z asked.

"I am holding audiences each day from now on, until all the Mortus living here have had a chance to come and see me, to witness for themselves that I am now their queen." Peony sat on the throne, her expression somewhat rueful. She was clad in blue shirt and pants—the outfit she had worn back in the assassins' den when she had been treating his injuries.

"You aren't going to try and abdicate?" Z asked, trying to keep his voice bland. If she gave up the crown, there was a chance he could be with her and get back into Heaven...

"No." She bit her lower lip, then sighed. "I don't think I can, to be honest. When they crowned me, it felt like my soul had been tied to Inferno."

He stared.

Tied to Inferno.

She had *become* part of Hell.

There was no way, if he started a romantic relationship with her, that he'd ever be accepted in Heaven. His heart twisted, the pain intense, like he'd been stabbed. Again. Z didn't know which thought brought the pain: the idea he couldn't get back into Heaven, or that he would have to walk away from Peony.

Pain flashed in her gaze as she watched him—could she sense the internal battle he fought?

"You don't need to stay with me," she said quietly. "You have your wings back, and you found your friend. I am a cambion who only wears this crown because I became a murderer." Tears made her eyes glassy, but she maintained eye contact.

"Why did you kill him?"

It was a question he should have asked earlier, would have asked earlier if he hadn't had complete faith in her inherent decency.

"He took pleasure in hurting others. Encouraged others to do it too, no doubt. I can sense the souls of every Mortus—I know who's been naughty or nice." A smile twisted her mouth. "But he wanted to hurt a woman he had almost killed the day before. If not for Lady Eramine and me, she'd have been dead. Hurting her once wasn't good enough for him. He wanted to do it all over again. I couldn't live with myself if I had done nothing. So I touched him."

All true.

"Death was too kind a punishment," Z said, leaning toward her.

"You're an angel, you don't need to lie to me."

"I'm not lying. I was a warrior before I was abducted. I've killed in the name of duty. Does that make me a murderer?"

Her face clouded over. "I don't know. Killing people isn't right."

"Sometimes, death is the only way to stop evil. And

sometimes, we will kill to protect those who can't do it for themselves."

The doors to the chamber opened, and Mortus demons filed into the room. Those at the front paused at the sight of the ash mounds, before weaving their way carefully around the piles.

"Weren't they meant to be cleaned up?" Z asked.

Godric and the older female demon came to stand beside Peony. "I thought it would give them a nice warning."

"The Mortus only respect power," the female demon said. "Peony is an abomination—a cambion. They will not respect her unless she proves she is stronger than them."

Z had a knife out and at the woman's throat in a second. "Don't you ever call her that again."

If he needed evidence he'd lost his mind, here it was. Almost skin-to-skin with a Mortus demon, all to protect another who was strong enough to turn them all to ash if she wanted.

A gentle hand touched his arm, and he lowered the weapon and stepped aside. "Z, it's okay."

He shook his head. "It's not."

"I am only saying what the Mortus think," the female snapped.

"What *you* think."

"Lady Eramine is my grandmother, Z. If she can't accept me," Peony nodded at the gathering Mortus, "they won't."

Her grandmother?

He couldn't see any resemblance, aside from the color of their irises. Although, those glacial gray eyes *did* remind him of Dru.

They turned to the crowd as the doors swing shut, sealing them all in. There was perhaps three hundred Mortus crammed into the room.

Peony gripped the arms of the throne and leaned forward, although she did not stand. "You will bow before your queen."

At first, no one moved, rebellion in every line of their bodies. But then, shockingly, Lady Eramine dropped to her knees, followed a microsecond later by Godric.

Gasps sounded throughout the crowd at the royals' actions, but soon others were bowing, until almost all of the Mortus were genuflecting before their new queen.

Peony flicked her hand, and Lady Eramine and Godric stood.

"Might is right in Hell," Peony's voice rang through the hall. "I killed King Alvin. I am also the daughter of Prince Clement. I rule the Mortus by this right."

Murmurs sounded, but she ignored them.

"Things are going to change. New laws will be made. But first, know this. The harems will no longer exist. The women are now free to live where they choose, go where they please. Any person seeking to have sexual relations with a female Mortus must first gain my permission— with the female Mortus present. Any sexual activities conducted without my approval will be met with immediate and harsh punishment. Any Mortus who abuses another in any way will also be punished."

Angry shouts now sounded, while the few women present huddled down on themselves.

"You're nothing but talk!" a Mortus shouted from the middle of the crowd.

Peony pointed at a gilded chair to her right. Her eyes turned the now-familiar inky black with green flames, and a second later ash rained down softly on the carpet. "I do not bluff. Fail to abide by my laws, and you will be punished."

Uncowed, a male who appeared to wear more gold than clothing, shouted, "I will not be ruled by an angel-lover!"

Peony glared at him, and for a moment, she appeared as cold and deadly as her sister. Z wanted to reach out and touch her, to bring back the warmth he knew she had. But to do so would weaken her in front of the audience, and that he was not willing to do.

"Who I am friends with is none of your business. But you forget your lore. The mother of our race was an angel."

"We are the children of Satan!"

"And an angel."

Truth. She spoke the truth.

Shock floored Z. *An angel* had helped create a race rumored to be so evil that even other demons feared them? Had the angel willingly offered her body to the ruler of Inferno?

"You lie!"

For a moment, he panicked and thought *he* had shouted that useless denial. But no, it was the gold-encrusted Mortus, along with several others.

"The writings in the halls state this. Your own den proclaims the truth. As do your legends."

"Lies!" The male rushed them, hands spread out like claws, rage making him appear manic.

Z stepped forward, wishing he had a sword in his

hand to defend her.

A blade of jade green flame burst to life, the hilt warm and alive, momentarily taking him aback. Then he swung it in a high arc, slicing it through the male's neck just as his body combusted, drizzling yet more ash onto the carpeted floor.

The blade vanished.

Surprise held him immobile for a brief moment, before he stepped back to Peony's side.

He had called forth his first blade!

Silence descended on the hall then, a silence filled with rage and hatred so intense it licked at his skin. But alongside those emotions, he could see a begrudging respect in the features of some of the Mortus. Peony was winning them over.

She raked the room with her eyes. "You are all dismissed. But make no mistake, if you fail to adhere to my rules, be prepared to find yourself in an urn for the rest of eternity."

The double doors at the rear of the room swung open, and the Mortus began leaving. Eventually, only Lady Eramine, Godric, Z and Peony remained.

He was...proud of her, he realized. She had not hesitated to protect his life, and those around her, when the Mortus had attacked. And she had set rules which he thought were only fair and just.

She will make a great queen.

One the Mortus needed.

A slow whistle sounded to his left, and Z spun on the balls of his feet, fist snapping out quickly in a punch.

Azrael dodged the blow, barely, and grinned. "You're getting quicker."

Z settled back. "Hmph."

"What was the whistle for?" Peony asked.

"You're almost as scary as my lady love. I was impressed." He turned to Z. "And you summoned a blade of fire."

"Lady love?" Godric sneered.

"Dru, of course."

Peony slumped a little at that. "Dru is scary in a crazy way."

Azrael grinned. "Yeah, it's great."

CHAPTER 35

They were back in the king's—Peony's—study.

Her body ached. She was exhausted, but too wired to sleep; so much had happened. She had broken her vow. Twice. Rage at her own weakness poured through her. She wasn't even sure how much time had passed, but it could have easily been a couple of days.

And the worst part?

Z was going to walk away from her.

Not today, maybe not tomorrow, but eventually he would leave. He had to. He was a fully-fledged angel with wings, and she was a cambion tied to Hell. They were doomed.

But she wanted him anyway.

Even if only for a day.

"Are you all right?" Z asked, leaning his hip against the stone desk.

Peony stared at the Orb, which just showed her Z's face again. It helped bolster her resolve. "Not really."

He moved closer, until his hands settled on her shoulders. Oh, how she loved the feel of him touching her, of his warmth seeping through her clothes to settle against her skin. She leaned up on her tip-toes and pressed her lips to his.

He pulled back slowly, reluctantly. "I am not sure this is a good idea."

Peony linked her arms behind his head. "I am. Z, I *need* this."

He had no idea how much, or how vulnerable it made her to admit that.

Z would be the only man she'd ever be able to touch. If this was her sole chance at intimacy, with a man she had grown to adore over the weeks she'd been healing him, then she'd take it.

No regrets.

Z's eyes turned a deep emerald so dark it was almost black, and he inhaled deeply, like he was memorizing her scent. "You are so beautiful."

She wanted to laugh, a little sadly. "You don't have to lie to me, just make out with me."

"I don't lie, and especially not about this."

Then he kissed her.

Desperate, hungry for more, Peony pressed herself against the hard lines of his body, feeling her heart pound as tingles formed in her belly...and lower. She shoved her hands between their chests, struggling to remove his shirt, so she could touch him, really touch him, for the first time.

How could one piece of clothing be so difficult to take off?

He ripped the shirt away, then pulled her close, kissing her deeply, his tongue imitating sex.

She pulled away, laughing with delight. Z's hands

grazed the bottom of her shirt. "Can I take it off?"

"Gods, yes."

Then she was just in her basic bra, the white cotton embarrassingly practical. But Z stared at her like she was magnificent. Peony spread her hands over his tanned skin, marveling at how smooth it was, how delicious. Then she was kissing his neck, tasting him as his pulse jerked wildly against her tongue, as his hands ran over her body, learning her curves.

This is what it's meant to be like.

Z pulled her mouth to his as one of his hands pushed past the waistband of her trousers. The kiss was hot, electric, and she felt like she might burst with sheer happiness from it. His other hand then cupped her breast, and she moaned when his finger swept over a hardened nipple. "Can I kiss you there?"

She nodded, and gasped when his mouth closed over her through the fabric. "Stop asking for permission."

As if she would deny him.

Her body was on fire as he sucked one nipple, then the other, into his mouth. She wanted to taste him again, but when she tugged on his hair, trying to pull him back for another kiss, he resisted. Instead, he trailed kisses down her torso, past her belly button, and to the apex of her thighs. Her breath left her in a whoosh.

Then his mouth was moving her over her panties. Embarrassment speared through her. She was so wet...what if he hated it?

He pulled back. "What's wrong?"

"I'm sorry, it's so..." she waved a hand awkwardly at her groin.

He grinned then, so hot and masculine, her knees

went weak. "Delicious?"

Heat seared her cheeks, but then his tongue licked the seam of her sex, and her mind went blank. Pleasure built as his tongue and mouth sucked and caressed her, and soon, her knees gave way. Z grabbed her, laid her on the study's floor. He was relentless, the sensation peaking, and she cried out, lights bursting on the back of her eyelids as ecstasy overwhelmed her.

Her whole body turned to liquid, and she relaxed in the aftermath of her first shared climax. Z crawled up her body then, pressing the hard length of his erection against her molten core. He gave her a teasing grin as she opened bleary eyes.

"I hope that was okay."

Bolder than she thought possible, she slid her hand down his torso until she cradled his hardness. "More than."

He made to roll away.

No.

She slid her hand up his length and he froze, chest heaving. "Peony?"

"I want this." She tightened her grip.

"I'm not sure—"

"I am."

Somehow, she managed to shove his trousers low enough to expose him, then she was spreading her legs, guiding the tip to where she ached. Z hissed at the contact.

A thought made her stop. "Do *you* want this?"

She needed to feel him. To be with him. But what if he didn't want her?

He lowered his forehead to touch hers. "More than

anything."

Then he slowly pushed forward, stretching her, making her ache with wanting. Z leaned his weight on one arm, then clasped one of her ungloved hands in his, their fingers entwining, the intimacy so intense she wanted to cry. He kissed her cheeks, and then slowly withdrew, before sliding back in, her body welcoming him with a firm squeeze.

"This is going to kill me," he muttered.

She laughed again.

"Laugh all you want, wench. I will have my revenge."

He was *teasing* her.

It was wonderful.

Then he was fully within her and he began to *move*.

Pleasure threatened to overload her senses, and she tilted her hips, meeting him thrust for thrust. Z was all she could see, all she could feel; she was part of him, and he was part of her. She didn't think she'd ever felt more complete. Then the pleasure spiked, so intense she screamed, his shout following hers soon after.

She lay beneath him, her heart pounding in time to his, and it was all she could do just to *breathe*.

Z brushed some of her hair from her forehead. "Are you okay?"

She answered as honestly as she could. "Never been better."

CHAPTER 36

Z didn't know up from down, good from bad, right from wrong. Everything he'd been taught was a lie—not all demons were evil. In fact, some demons were more 'good' than angels.

Case in point: Peony was a better person than him.

She had given herself freely, with no expectation, just welcome arms and the taste of love on her tongue. Could he have done the same, given their respective situations?

He wasn't so sure.

But he knew one thing: he couldn't leave her now, if only because making love with her had been just that—making love. The pleasure he had reached in her arms had made the satisfaction he'd found with Dina pallid.

Also, he couldn't leave her because she was his better half, and she planned to make a new life for herself here, and she'd need help. Someone to watch over her. A *partner*.

A life in Heaven, where he would be forever marginalized because of the color of his wings wasn't the life he wanted. He could fight here, every day, by trying to make the Mortus a little less evil.

A fool's errand.

But one he would do, if Peony were by his side.

She stirred in his arms, her satin-smooth skin sliding against his. "Should we find the others?"

"No."

She laughed joyously, then stood and grabbed her clothes, hiding her naked body, still self-conscious. He wanted to tell her that it was okay, he relished the sight of her, but he didn't want to make her uncomfortable. This was all so new to her.

And him.

He hadn't ever made love before. What was the protocol?

Peony made quick work of dressing and turned, stopping short at the sight of him sprawled on the rug. He would have flexed his biceps if they weren't such sad excuses for muscles. Giving himself a mental shake—he would regain his former build—he threw his clothes on as well.

"Do you know what Azrael has been doing, while he's been waiting for Dru?" Peony asked.

He shook his head. The other Dart had been conspicuously absent for the majority of their time in the Mortus den. Z had a feeling it was because the other angel was playing matchmaker.

After they left the study, Peony reached out shyly and took his hand. Twining their fingers together like teenagers, they walked down the halls, toward the harem's communal area. Peony didn't particularly like leaving the room for too long, just in case Dru returned there before them. She was worried her sister would kill first and ask questions later, especially considering what the den had been like when she'd arrived.

Once there, she stopped next to one of the ash piles. "I feel guilty."

"Why? They were dead."

"They died because of me."

"They chose their actions."

She let go of his hand and wrapped her arms around his torso, hugging him. Trick's brand on his stomach burned at the contact. For a moment, he was stunned by the sheer trust she had in him, then he held her close, breathing in the sugar-and-cinnamon scent of her.

A crackle of electricity made him tense. Looking down into her eyes, wondering what had upset her, he saw nothing but pure gray.

Releasing her, he turned around, only to be slammed to the floor, a heavy weight pinning him down.

As his face was ground into a pile of ash, he shouted, "Peony!"

She screamed, "Let him go!"

Instead, his arms were wrenched behind his back, his wings crushed in the process. "You're coming with us, angel-boy," snarled a rough voice he didn't recognize.

Had Trick sent people to steal him back?

I will not be taken again.

Summoning the blade of fire to his constrained hands, he grinned at the resulting grunt of pain. The grip on his wrists loosened, and he spun out of the hold, jumping to his feet and spreading his wings for balance.

Infernus.

Three of the demons were in the hall, one with a cauterized wound on his torso, and two holding Peony by the arms. Too bad her long sleeves had prevented their instant deaths.

"Are you okay?" he called to her.

She nodded, her expression tight.

"What do you want?" Z demanded.

One of the Infernus holding Peony spoke: "We want you. Come with us, and we won't have to hurt the girl." Electricity arced over the huge demon's wings.

Peony's reply was authoritative, "If you leave this instant, I'll let you live."

They laughed.

"You? We heard about you, healer girl. You can't hurt a fly." The demon wrenched her arm up.

I'm going to rip off his limb as punishment.

"I warned you," Peony said, and her eyes swirled with darkness. Clearly, the Infernus hadn't spotted the coronet around her forehead, or realized what it meant for them, standing in the Mortus den.

The Infernus next to Z lunged, claws grabbing onto his wing and digging in. The pain was instant and fiery, and he gritted his teeth, fighting the urge to wrench the wing away. That would just cause more damage, and he wasn't sure how quickly it would heal.

The demon's fingers slid over the fine filaments of jade in his feathers.

Then a harsh curse filled the air, and the grip on his wings slackened.

The Infernus collapsed to the ground, thrashing against the carpet, foam spitting from his mouth. A second later, he was dead.

"What the fuck did you do?" one of the other Infernus shouted, digging his claws into Peony's delicate arm.

Z had no idea. Had his wing *poisoned* the demon?

"Just grab the angel and go!"

The new voice made Z swing around.

He didn't recognize the demon's face, but he *knew* that voice. It was from one of his abductors.

The two demons holding Peony let go and launched themselves at Z. He ducked and wove, kicking and slicing with his flame sword where he could. He grunted when he missed a block, a fist ramming hard into his stomach. The air left his lungs in a rush, but he ignored the discomfort and slashed an opponent on the arm with the blade. The stench of burning flesh rose around him.

"*Grab him!*"

Z was tripped, then pinned to the ground, a starburst of pain making him giddy as his nose broke. Peony screamed his name.

Have to save her. Have to save me.

But two massive weights held him down, and he was too weak to throw them off.

"Get off him!" Peony shouted.

The air around him intensified, as a spell took shape. They were trying to teleport him away.

I can't leave her.

One moment, the air was sizzling with power, the next, ash drifted down on him. He lay there, panting for a second, before leaping to his feet, blade out.

Peony strode forward, her eyes a deep darkness. "Bad form, Kerrington. Coming to steal what isn't yours."

She knew the demon's name?

"We just need to borrow him." The demon spread his hands out, palms up. "Then he can go back to Trick."

She shook her head. "No deal."

"I'm not asking for permission." Kerrington lunged at Z. "He's coming with me."

But now it was just Kerrington versus Z and Peony, they would win.

I want him taken alive.

Z darted to the side, just as Peony stepped closer, eyes burning.

"Don't ash him!" he shouted.

But just as Z sprang to grapple with the demon, Kerrington toppled to the ground, his leathery wings flailing. There was a knife embedded in one of his eyes.

"*What—*?"

Who?

Damnit!

Z needed answers, and the demon could have provided them...

"You're welcome!" Dru called.

"I totally had that kill!" Azrael shouted from the other side of the room.

Inspecting the body more closely, Z noticed two more knife hilts protruding from the demon's back.

Death from both sides.

He growled in frustration.

"My knife made the kill," Dru said, and Z did a double take at the sight of her. Her white hair was smeared with blood and gore, and her face sported a black eye and a split lip. Her clothing was torn, and gashes scored her body.

Azrael was by her side in an instant, his hands gentle as he ran them over her body, checking the wounds. "What the Hell happened to you?"

"Fucking Metcalf."

"Metcalf did that?" Peony asked, eyes shifting back to gray.

The imp limped over and began prodding the Infernus' limp form. "Hey! Don't blame me. I didn't cut her up."

"If you hadn't touched my ring, we wouldn't have ended up in Sheol surrounded by a bunch of Reynard's Imps," Dru said.

Metcalf raised glimmering black eyes. "It was glorious."

"Glorious? I nearly got turned into lunch!"

"But we killed so many of them. My family didn't know what hit them."

"Yes they did—they knew it was you," Dru grumbled.

"You're right. It was great."

Peony's sister shook her head. "Fucking cannibal."

Metcalf looked pleased.

"Actually," a cold voice said, interrupting the banter, "the kill was mine."

Godric.

I hadn't even realized the demon was in the room.

Either Z was getting lax, or the Mortus was that sneaky. He had a feeling it was the latter.

They all turned to the demon as he strode toward them and plucked one of the daggers from the Infernus' back. He cleaned the blade on the dead male's pants.

"Metcalf! Don't eat that!" Dru slapped the imp's hand away from Kerrington's corpse.

"What?" The imp rubbed his wrist. "I've never had Infernus before."

"And you aren't about to start now."

"You are seriously a buzz kill. Peony would let me."

The Mortus queen turned slightly green. "Uhh..."

"Just burn the body and be done with it," Azrael said.

"Burn the body?" Dru glanced around the room and frowned when she spotted the piles of ash. "How many Infernus attacked you?"

"Oh, these are mostly Mortus," Godric said, slipping his blade away.

"Who killed them?"

Frosted gray eyes glanced over them. "You, them, me, Peony..."

"*Peony*?"

The healer winced. "Only some of the Infernus, and two of the Mortus."

"Some of the Infernus? What the Hell happened?"

Azrael ran a hand over his mate's arm. "I'll explain later."

"You better."

Godric kicked Metcalf's hand, which had somehow made its way back to the corpse. "And don't burn the bodies. Not yet, anyway."

"Why not?" Peony asked, her expression sad and grim.

Godric smiled mirthlessly "Because we need to send a little message."

CHAPTER 37

Godric opened the door and Peony stopped on the threshold. When she'd asked if the den had the Internet, she hadn't expected him to whisk her and Z away to a room that looked like a state-of-the-art government installation. There were LCD screens everywhere, along with a huge server in the back, and a bunch of herbs and skulls lining the walls. A desk wrapped around three walls of the room, and it was packed with high-tech equipment, most of which Peony couldn't name.

"The Internet requires sacrifices and spells, at least in Inferno," Godric said, noticing where she was looking.

She shuddered. At least none of the skulls looked human or demon.

Peony walked into the room and took a seat on one of the swivel chairs. "Do you have Skype?"

He stared at her. "Skype?"

"You know—"

"Of course, I know. You think I have this set up and I don't know what fucking Skype is?" The demon shook his head and opened a laptop that had been sitting on a desk. "Here. Who do you want to call?"

Peony wiped a hand over her face. "Trick."

Z tensed beside her, and she laid a gentle hand on his arm.

"The asshole who sold you?" Godric rubbed a hand over his chin. "He lied to us."

She shrugged. "Yeah, but that's Trick. If he can screw you over, he will."

"Why do you want to call him?"

"How about you just do what your queen asks of you?" Peony snapped.

Fake it till you make it.

It had been her motto in the throne room, and whenever she spoke to the Mortus. In fact, she had decided to channel Dru. Her sister wouldn't have put up with any of their attitude, and the Mortus seemed to respect her for it. But it didn't change how she felt—guilt and shame for breaking a promise she'd made to herself, sorrow for taking lives, no matter that she had done it to protect first Milly and then Z.

"As Your Highness wishes."

The Skype dial-tone sounded and then the video feed kicked in. Trick appeared, his golden hair disheveled and chocolate-brown eyes suspicious. He wouldn't be expecting a call from the Mortus king's address. "To what do I owe the pleasure of—wait, *Peony*?"

"Hi, Trick." She waved, giving him a small, twisted smile. "You were expecting someone else?"

She stared at the computer screen hard, but it didn't show her Trick's aura, which was a shame. She would have loved the extra information—she might have even been able to work out his species.

Her former slave-master frowned. "Why do you have a crown on?"

"Oh this?" She waved a hand at her head. "I killed the king and now I'm queen. You know, the usual."

He blinked at her. Then said slowly, "*You* killed the king?"

She turned to look at Z and Godric. "Did I mumble? I thought I was clear."

"Sounded clear to me," Z replied.

Trick spluttered. "Is that—?"

"The angel you had stashed away that recently went AWOL? Why, yes it is."

She was perhaps enjoying this conversation a bit too much.

"*Peony*—"

"That tone doesn't work on me anymore. I don't answer to you."

"No, but he does." Trick pointed at Z.

"No, he doesn't."

"He's a blood slave. I *own* him."

"Fraudulently obtained," Peony snapped.

"It's his thumbprint on the contract."

That was true, she'd seen them pressing his thumb on it.

Z leaned toward the screen. "I am not your slave."

"Yes, you are. Unless you can find me another angel, you're mine."

No.

But it was true. She'd been a blood slave, she knew how the system worked. A life for a life.

"This isn't why I called," Peony said. They would find a way to free Z later.

"No?" Trick settled back from the screen, returning to his usual sarcastic self.

Ass.

"I need to borrow Opal."

"There is no borrowing. You can only hire." A flicker of greed flashed across his handsome features.

"Opal said she owed me."

"Fuck. I'm going to wring her neck. She should know better than to say that."

"Please wait to murder her until after she visits me."

Godric snorted in the background.

"Why are you even asking me?" Trick asked.

"Because I'm the ruler of the Mortus. It's polite."

Her former master shook his head. "Polite will get you killed."

"Thanks for the advice. I think I'll ignore it." She turned to the side, as if she were going to leave. "Oh, and Trick?"

"Yes." He sounded like he was grinding his teeth.

"The Infernus tried to steal Z back. Thought you might want to know."

She hung up to the sound of Trick cursing. Resettling herself in the chair, she muttered, "Now, I need to call my mom."

A few hours later, Opal rubbed her hands together as she stared at Peony. The Radiato demon's aura was black. "You're the new Mortus queen? No one believes it."

Peony rolled her eyes. "They had better."

Opal sniggered. "So, what can I do for you? Trick said

you were calling in a favor. He was so annoyed, it was wonderful."

Her friends really had socialization issues.

Peony motioned to Z, who was leaning against a bookshelf in her study. "Can you have a look at him with your X-ray vision and tell me if you see anything unusual?"

The Infernus' raid had been bothering her. Why had they come for Z, knowing that Trick would retaliate with the full force of the guild if they were caught? There weren't that many demons who were foolish enough to take on the Halcyon Guild.

Opal tilted her head to the side. "That's it? And define 'unusual'. The dude has wings."

"Unusual, aside from him being an angel."

"Right." Opal leaned in close to Peony and whispered, "You do know it's super-weird you're friends with an angel?"

"I'm friends with Metcalf."

The Radiato demon pursed her lips and nodded. "Fair point."

Then Opal *looked* at Z. She was still and silent for a good two minutes, and Z started to sweat. From the radiation? Worry spiked inside her.

How well was he, after his recovery?

"Are you done?" Peony asked, concerned.

"Yes. The guy is fine, aside from being overweight."

"*Overweight?*" Z's voice was strangled.

Well, Opal had different standards.

"Nothing else?" Peony prodded.

Maybe her theory had been too crazy.

"He's fine. Aside from the lump of stone in his

abdomen, he's good as gold."

Excitement shot through her, but she tried to keep her expression blank. "Thanks, Opal."

"That was it?" The demon looked disappointed. "You saved my life. I had hoped for something a little more grand."

"I needed to make sure he wasn't suffering from any health issues. You know me, I can't stop being a doctor, even after being crowned."

The skeletal demon lowered her voice, concern written over her features. "Were you worried because he's fat?"

Peony bit the inside of her cheek to keep from laughing. "Yes."

"Ahhh." The Radiato nodded sagely.

"Can you keep this visit quiet?" Peony asked.

"Of course."

"Blood swear it?"

Suspicion crept into Opal's gaze.

"Do you want people to know you helped an angel?" Peony asked. "This way you can't admit it, even to Trick."

"Hells no. That's a good idea."

Minutes after the oath was sworn and Peony had bandaged the cut on her forearm from completing the ritual, Opal left, ushered out by Godric.

When they were alone, Z sat down in one of the chairs set before the desk. "I have a *rock* in my stomach?" Z asked, running a hand over his face.

"Apparently."

"Do you know what it is?" he asked, eyes shadowed.

"I have an idea. Let me make a call."

CHAPTER 38

Z looked around the Mortus infirmary, wincing; the scent of antiseptic brought back unpleasant memories. A laptop was set up on a trolley, the screen showing a close-up of Selene, Peony's mother. To the left of the trolley, the god Osiris stood, looking surprisingly suave in a set of blue medical clothing—scrubs, Peony called them.

"Why is he here, again?" Z asked.

It was bad enough that Peony wanted to operate on him, let alone having a deposed god in the room while she did it.

"Oz is a pathologist," Selene said from the computer.

Z frowned, unsure what that meant. Warriors in Heaven didn't have a lot of time for human occupations.

"He performs autopsies," Peony said.

"He works on dead bodies?" Z asked. *That* one, he was familiar with.

"The anatomy is the same, dead or alive," Osiris said, his voice bland.

The door to the infirmary opened, admitting Azrael and Dru. "Sorry we're late," Dru said. "Do we trust this guy?" She pointed at the god.

"I vouch for him," Selene said.

Peony nodded.

Z didn't trust the god, but he *did* trust Peony.

Once the door closed, Osiris snapped his fingers, and gold fire licked up the walls of the room. "The silence spell will last until the door is opened again."

That was useful.

"Are you ready?" Peony placed a hand on Z's arm, her fingers briefly squeezing his bicep. Her touch steadied him.

Nodding, he climbed onto the bench, and lifted the 'gown' they had given him, while Peony placed a sheet over his waist. He laid back, careful of his wings. Taking a deep breath, he held it for a few seconds before exhaling.

"Are we going to anesthetize him?" Osiris asked.

Z flinched. The last time he had been knocked out, it had ended badly for him and for the Darts. "I want to be awake."

The god frowned. "I can do a spinal tap."

Peony watched him with steady eyes. "I recommend it."

Holding her look, he nodded.

"You'll need to sit up."

"You brought all the appropriate medications and equipment?" Peony asked.

"I don't need to." The god smiled and suddenly there was a second trolley in the room, covered in plastic packaging and more blue sheets.

"Handy trick," Dru murmured.

"How long can you stay here?" Selene asked.

"Long enough. Let's be quick."

Within seconds, Z was sitting again. A prick in his back spoke of a local anesthetic, then he was told to hold still for a few seconds. Soon, he was being taped up.

"Lie down." Osiris helped guide him back to a prone position, and then the sensation below his sternum began to deaden. The god held up a little packet. "This is ice, tell me when it's cold and when it's not."

The test quickly proved that he was numb in all the right places.

"Let's get started."

Z closed his eyes and focused on his breathing as fluid was wiped across his stomach. Then all he could feel was pressure, as someone began to operate on his abdomen.

You are pathetic. You should watch.

Yes, possibly. But he had no desire to see his innards exposed to the air, to know that this was happening because he'd been weak in the first place.

"This is gross," Dru muttered.

"You see this kind of thing all the time," Peony muttered.

"Not when people are *alive*."

"That makes a difference?"

"Apparently."

He almost didn't mind the bickering—it made the experience feel strangely normal.

A few more seconds ticked by and then Osiris spoke, "I see."

"What?" Z asked, opening his eyes but keeping his stare fixed on the ceiling.

"I'm taking a photo, and then I recommend we close," the god said. "Here, Selene, see?"

Z turned to the laptop, and saw Osiris holding his phone up to the camera. The dark-haired woman nodded. "Yes, close him up."

"We leave it there?" Peony asked.

"Yes."

Fifteen minutes later, he was stitched back up, and the anesthetic was removed. Sensation came back surprisingly quickly, leaving him with an ache in his stomach. Compared to the pain he had suffered for the past several months, he could ignore it.

Osiris then turned the phone toward him. In a web of flesh lay a jagged piece of stone—clear like a diamond. Z's veins and sinews seemed to have become attached to it.

"I really have a stone in me."

"Not just any stone," the god said. "That is a primordial artifact."

"Do you know which one?" Azrael asked.

No, it can't be.

All this time...

"Heaven's Heart," Peony said.

"You *knew*?" Azrael spun toward Peony. Z held out a hand, drawing her closer to him.

"I had a theory." She looked at the ground. "When I asked the Orb where the stolen piece was, it kept showing me Z. I thought it was showing me *my* heart." Her cheeks blazed with color.

She's embarrassed.

"He is your mate," Osiris said. "It was a logical conclusion."

"All right, but now we've found it, shouldn't we have removed it?" Azrael asked.

Selene shook her head. "It is hidden where it is. Since Z is not dead, it will not harm him any further."

"What do you mean?"

"An artifact like this shouldn't be housed in flesh it hasn't chosen; if it is, it will slowly kill the vessel unless it's removed. You, however, seem healthy enough."

So it had been Heaven's Heart that was killing him? Not a demon poison.

"I was healed by a witch."

"No matter how powerful the witch, she wouldn't have been able to heal you unless the Heart had accepted its new home." The god clicked his fingers, and the surgical equipment vanished.

"That's why the Infernus were after you," Peony said. "They want the Heart back."

So did the archangels. They would have to tell the other Darts about this, and fast.

We have the first piece. One out of three—already they had beaten the odds. *Only two more pieces to go, and the others can have their wings back.*

Osiris stepped forward and kissed Z's forehead. His skin burned where the god's lips touched it, and the tingle of magic washed through him, making the handprint on his torso burn.

"Uh, Selene, your god-buddy is coming on to Z," Dru called.

"It's the kiss of death," Selene replied.

"What?" Peony leaped forward just as Osiris stepped back.

"You are now one of mine. The tracking spell the Infernus laid on you is gone, and if you are in danger, I'll know. I can't do anything about the blood-bond, though." The god's citrine eyes turned hard. "I don't do this often, so don't make me regret it."

Z nodded. "Thank you."

Whoever heard of an angel tied to a deposed god? But it was done now.

"How many Infernus know about the Heart, do you think?" Z asked, but he knew none of them would be able to answer.

Azrael's voice was low as he replied, "We will just have to wait and see."

"But what do we do about them for now?" Dru asked, playing with a knife that had suddenly appeared in her hands.

"Don't worry," Peony said with a smile. "I have a plan for that."

CHAPTER 39

Peony sat at her desk, one of her fancier crowns on her head. Crafted from platinum and encrusted with diamonds, it was heavy; she had the beginnings of a headache. She still wore her scrubs, though, and had her hair tied back in a bun. She wasn't going to change who she was entirely for the Mortus; but she could put on one Hell of a show. And she wanted to let her incoming guest know that she wasn't your typical demon.

"Do you think he'll come?" Z asked.

"He'll come."

Her mate stood behind her, a solid presence that gave her comfort. He was dressed in leathers, with knives and daggers strapped to his body. He was looking healthier than he had since she had begun treating him, and he was so handsome it hurt to watch him.

He was leaving her.

But not today.

A bell chimed, and then a man appeared in the middle of the room, facing the desk. He was handsome, and wore a tailored business suit, the shirt open at the collar. His mahogany hair was swept back from his face, and his black eyes were empty.

"You are not what I expected," the new arrival said silkily.

"I am often surprising," Peony replied, and fought to keep her expression calm. The man's power pulsed against her skin, and his aura glowed golden—like Osiris' had.

Satan, the ruler of Inferno, had the aura of a god.

"Would you like to sit?" she asked.

"What? No bow? I *am* the ruler of this realm." He glided gracefully forward and sat in one of the two brown leather chairs opposite her desk.

"I thought we could be more relaxed, since we're family."

Shit. What if he's a real stickler for protocol?

No, go with your gut.

Show no weakness. But be polite, be courteous, and be firm. That had been her mother's advice. *Murder someone if you have to.* That had been Dru's.

She'd stick to Plan A for now.

"Thank you for responding to my invitation," Peony said, her hands clasped together on the desk's surface, in front of a keyboard. She'd had the office upgraded to include technology—another sign she wasn't like the old king.

"It was difficult to ignore. The Mortus king deposed? A queen ruling in his stead? This was too interesting to leave alone. Especially since the Mortus are mine."

I am not yours, Peony wanted to scream, but she couldn't deny what the writings in the halls told her. The Mortus were the children of Heaven and Hell, and Peony was their queen. But unlike the regular Mortus, she was also a child of the Human Realm.

"I killed my uncle, it's true." She nodded at a brass urn that sat on a bookshelf to her right—a sign of dishonor in Hell. "And I have been bound to Inferno."

"Nonsense," he narrowed his eyes. "Only I am bound to Hell."

Peony opened her hand, and dancing green flames burst to life in the air above her palm. Satan stared at them for a moment, disbelief etched into his expression as he studied the Hellfire. Then slowly, he smiled. It made her skin crawl. "You are the true heir of the Mortus."

"So it has been foretold, and so it has come to be," Peony said. Godric had told her that she *must* use that phrase when Satan realized what she was.

Finally, the Hell-lord's gaze came to rest on Z, his expression turning scornful. "You mated with *an angel*?"

"Don't be hypocritical, Grandfather." Peony smiled then, wondering where the courage came from. She could almost hear Dru cheering for her in the background.

Keep it up. Be like Dru, just for a few more minutes.

Satan flicked an invisible piece of lint from his sleeve. "Ah, but I didn't *mate* with her. Just fucked her."

"Fate, it is fickle, isn't it?"

"I won't be ruled by fate. And you should follow in my footsteps, if you wish to stay queen."

"I'll stay queen, and I'll do it my way."

"I see you've already begun. I have some very angry Infernus complaining that an upstart cambion has slain one of their own. Then this cambion had the audacity to send them the head of their fallen, along with a menacing note."

"The Infernus came here and threatened my mate," Peony said. "They are lucky the Mortus did not declare war. And you know, Grandfather, that if the Mortus go to war, then you would have to support us, even though the Infernus are also your children."

The Infernus were Lucifer's and Satan's, whereas the Mortus were solely Satan's.

The conflict would pit Lucifer against Satan. Sheol against Inferno.

It was a no-win situation for her race's ancestor.

The Hell-lords were not meant to war against each other, except when their direct descendants were at risk.

"I will have a talk to the Infernus, and Lucifer. The Infernus will be warned your angel is off-limits." Satan curled his lip at the word 'angel'.

She nodded.

His dark eyes lingered on Z. "I've heard a rumor there is a black-winged angel hiding in Hell. Female. Vicious. Have you lost one of your own?"

"No angel is ever truly lost," Z replied, but Peony could feel the tension radiating from him.

"What a nice saying." The Hell-lord stood and rolled his eyes. "I will go clean up your mess, Granddaughter. No thanks required."

"None given."

Barking a laugh, Satan vanished.

Peony sagged in her chair.

Z's palm stroked over her shoulder. "You were brilliant."

She reached up to stroke the back of his hand. "Thank you."

He moved around the side of her chair, cupping her

cheek. "You amaze me every day."

"Could there really be a black-winged angel?" Peony asked.

Z frowned. "Dina is still missing. There's a chance it could be her."

"I can look for her in the Orb." Peony reached a hand out to her desk drawer, but stopped when Z touched her forearm.

She looked down. "When do you need to go?"

He drew his hand away. "Soon. Trick won't leave it alone. He has started ramping the pain up in the mark."

She closed her eyes.

I love you.

But she couldn't bind him to her with those words.

"We can still see each other," he said.

"Why won't you go back to Heaven, to tell them about your condition? I am sure they would break the contract with Trick."

"I need to give the other Darts time to find the next two pieces of the Heart. We want to approach Heaven with all three, so they can't say that I returned one piece, and them two."

She nodded. It made sense—especially if you didn't entirely trust those making the rules.

"Plus, I don't want to go back to Heaven."

Her eyes flew to his.

"I love you, and if I return, I will never see you again. They won't allow our relationship."

Peony shook her head. Surely he hadn't just said he loved her? That he was giving up Heaven to be with her?

"Don't be crazy. You're an angel. You belong in Heaven."

He gently pulled her to her feet. "When an angel's feathers become highlighted with color, it's their destiny. No angel has green-tinted feathers. None ever has. And no angel's wings have ever become poisonous, either."

She grimaced.

Look what her touch had done to him.

She had *ruined* him.

He stroked a hand down her neck. "You saved my life. You inspire me, and I want to be worthy of you. If I go to Trick, then I can still see you. He won't be able to prevent it without starting a diplomatic incident."

Peony threw her arms around his neck, pressing her cheek against his heart, needing to feel him. "You must not give up your future for me."

He kissed the top of her head, shaking his head. "Don't you see? You *are* my future."

EPILOGUE

Z smoothed his hands over Peony's back, reveling in the feel of her, the sense that she was his, and he was hers.

"I love you," she whispered.

He kissed her, tasting tears on her lips.

I will buy my freedom from Trick in record time.

The door banged open and Z raised his head, glowering at Godric.

"She insisted," the demon growled, and slammed the door shut behind him.

Seraphina stood in his place.

"I have a solution," she announced, striding forward. She wore loose black pants and a T-shirt that was strapped down with weapons. He had never seen her dressed so informally.

"To what?" Peony asked, turning her head so her cheek was pressed against his chest.

"The blood slave issue."

"There is no solution," Z said. "I will go there, and I will earn my freedom."

Seraphina tossed her head, sending hundreds of tiny

braids flying. "You have just found your mate, and in your...condition, we don't think it is wise that you be placed in the hands of the guild."

He couldn't argue with those points, but he had no option. "There is no way out of the deal."

"A life for a life," Peony said quietly.

Z tightened his arms around Peony, feeling her love and support wash through him.

"Exactly," Seraphina said. "He wants another angel. He can have one."

She met their stares defiantly. "He can have me."

ACKNOWLEDGMENTS

This book has been a bit of a whirlwind event, courtesy of the birth of my daughter, Maeve. Arriving early, she's kept me on my toes! Firstly, I'd like to thank my husband Tom, who gave me the time to write this book, while we had a newborn baby demanding many snuggles. I also want to thank my wonderful beta readers Joanne Danton and Kel Carpenter, and my eagle-eyed editor Pete Kempshall. As always, you are invaluable in the creation of my work.

Amanda Pillar is an USA TODAY Bestselling Author and award-winning editor who lives in Victoria, Australia, with her husband, daughter, and two cats.

Amanda has had numerous short stories published and has co-edited six fiction anthologies and solo-edited two.

Amanda's first novel, *Graced*, was published by Momentum in 2015. The stories *Captive* and *Survivor* were also released in 2016, followed by *Bitten* and *Ashes* in 2017. She has also just launched the Heaven's Heart series.

In her day job, she works as an archaeologist.